The Victorian Album

The Victorian Album

EVELYN BERCKMAN

Doubleday & Company, Inc.
Garden City, New York

The Victorian Album

I collect Victorian photographs. I mean I used to collect them, in circumstances very different from now—well, never mind that till later. But people forget, maybe, what accomplished photographers the Victorians were, from about 1840, and what thousands of their photographs, tens of thousands perhaps, survive. We forget too at our remove of time or perhaps can't imagine how much of a *craze* the camera became—and not only a craze; pundits began saying, *From this day on, painting is dead*—predictions of that sort. Almost at once Victoria appointed her own photographers, and had plenty to say about their skill or lack of skill, I promise you. She was well qualified to criticize of course, being no mean artist herself, far above the amateur level; if you don't believe me look at her line drawing of the Empress Eugénie in profile, or her painting of an Indian attendant. Oh yes, it took a good likeness to satisfy her, and I'm the same; I adore a likeness.

Now by likeness I mean people in their true character, not as the photographer instructed them to look. Not like us, showing all our teeth in a witless ecstasy as if at sight of some heavenly goal long despaired of and at last attained; no, Victorians scowled or glowered at the camera if the spirit moved them, they snubbed or reproved or disdained it. This is why we *see* these people; not as smiling masks touched-up and prettified, but *as they were*. Oh how those grave mutton-chopped husbands and rigid respectable wives would have withered the photographer who told them to 'look pleasant'.

So that, to me, is the first outstanding thing about those

portraits—the absence of the disguising smile. The second is a certain expression on women's faces, above all those women of the well-off, lower middling classes. That heavy look of boredom, that vacuity of lazy, waited-on, purposeless lives—terrifying! With four to six servants even in households by no means wealthy; with no need to lift a finger, with no occupation but to knit or embroider or make things to put under glass bells—flower-pieces of beads, shells or wax, of paper or fish-bones (fish-bone flowers are gospel, a Mrs. Dards made them her life-work); what vitality or intention could those faces show? Many of them stodgy with over-feeding as well, even young girls, for their other chief resource was eating. How they ate, those men and women, how they ate! Chops and kedgeree for breakfast, rich salmis for lunch, butter-soaked crumpets and plum-cake for tea, 'plain family dinners' of five to seven courses, washed down with a couple of bottles of port or sherry; all those defenceless stomachs and livers glutted, clogged with heavy food! Remember that disgusting young man, Charles Bravo, vomiting after the poison a quantity more suggestive of a mastodon than a man; remember also that the women of that day had no considerations of vanity to restrain them, big busts and swelling haunches being fashionable and admired. I've even a theory that the classic murders among the well-to-do of the period (like the Kent case, for example) had their origins in that smothering idleness and gross over-feeding.

But the third and most striking thing in those photographs—which only dawned on me after I'd seen hundreds—was the disproportion of men to women, or the other way about if you like. In group after group you'll find it, the lone male submerged in voluminous crinolines, like a solitary victim of shipwreck about to go down for the third time. The heavy wife; three, four or five over-plump young girls; the portly old dame in the elaborate widow's cap, either *his* mother or *her* mother; the stringy female with her vague aura of failure, either the husband's or the wife's unmarried sister. And all those idle useless daughters having to be well dowered, or no husband; the standard arranging of young lives by their wise, their so-wise elders. . . .

At this point I'm always so angry I've got to stop for seeing red; moreover I always will be angry, I can't leave off being angry, and what's more I don't apologize for being angry. A young life, managed by blundering hands, is the most defenceless thing there is. That these blunders are made by parents or teachers, with the very best of intentions, doesn't make them less injuriously lethal in the end. With well-meaning wrong-headedness, with self-opinionated complacence they'll distort or destroy your life, and at fifteen or sixteen how can you protect yourself? How could I, a young girl of my generation? I always knew exactly what I should do; my instinctive knowledge of my abilities was absolutely sound. I wanted to go to a trade-school when I'd left boarding-school, for even that early my interests were sharply channelled; I knew in what direction I should go and what training I needed. But no, the idea of a trade-school offended my parents, so after some tearful battles in which I was (of course) the loser, I went off to an expensive and snobbish establishment from which I emerged with ladylike snippets of this and that and no real mastery of anything whatever.

If I'd been allowed to follow my bent I'd be, today (or like to think I'd be) a competent textile designer. Instead, I'm a plain seamstress doing alterations rather than dressmaking, since alterations are what I'm offered mostly. Yes, thanks to my family's ruinous ideas of 'education' that's all the good I've had from my capacities, outside of the passion for reading I've retained—the useless passion.

And out of this constant reading I've found—will you believe it—an amazing thing: the degree of bitterness, the *unforgiving* bitterness, with which the greatest people who've ever lived look back on injuries done them in childhood or youth. Take Erasmus, the invited guest of kings and cities, the man who changed the thinking of his time; none of his grown-up glory helped him bear the thought of his illegitimacy, his childhood poverty, his tyrannical teachers who wasted years of his youth with their incompetence. Or take later names at random, take Swift or Dr. Johnson, take Edison's unsoftened memory of the man whose blow deafened him in one ear, take Edith Sitwell's unassuaged horror of her parents' deforming atmosphere; all their later fame didn't console them or soften them toward the authors of their early mishandling. Well, if these great ones couldn't forget or forgive it, a greater degree of high-mindedness can't be expected from someone like me, surely? from a nobody who knows just how much of a nobody she is?

Well now, as to my remaining interests if any, I've a minor and secret one: spiritualism. Smile if you like, and if you smile I'll know you're bigoted and ignorant, both. Strange inexplicable things happen and have always happened, but the whole subject has been so overlaid by fraud and trickery that of course one's inclined to despise or dismiss it, rather than trouble to examine the solid and authenticated instances. I myself've only known one person who has actually *seen* things, twice; one of my customers, the most delightful and intelligent woman employed in the foreign news service of the BBC, so don't go talking about low mentality or credulousness or anything of that sort. My own powers don't run to actual seeing (and I'm very glad of it) but long ago I realized I was a sensitive, and I joined one of the classes held by a medium for what we call *sitting for development*. A genuine medium, by the way, can always pick from any assembly the ones who have done so. But I gave it up rather soon, and in a hurry, and I'll tell you why. It was such a small thing, yet so *tremendous*. I was walking home one evening in November on a quite busy street with good lighting and a clear sky overhead; I mention this just so you won't visualize fog-bound fantasies, thank you very much. But all at once I realised that something had happened to me, I was walking in a sort of otherness, in a vacuum of silence, though the noises of traffic and so forth must have been going on all the time. And out of this strange enclosure of silence and remoteness I looked across the road at something, and for one instant—I swear this to you—I couldn't imagine at all what it was. Then the strangeness dissolved completely, and do you know what it turned out to be, the object of my bewilderment? *Houses*, that's all, just a row of ordinary terrace houses. But apparently, and quite without knowing it, I'd progressed so far in development that for one moment the real world—or what we call the real world—was unreal to me; as unreal as if I'd come from another planet, where houses were unknown.

So I gave up my sessions for development in a hurry. If you're living on this planet you're *on* it, for better or worse—stuck with it as they say—so no use to cultivate faculties that estrange you from it so violently that you can't get your bearings; hard enough managing to exist under familiar conditions. But now that I've tried to describe the experience, I see how completely I've failed—failed to convey that chill of *otherness*, that terror of dislocation in time and space; as though you'd been swept up without warning and dropped in an unknown desert. No, you can't feel the horror, the awful alienness, till it happens to you. And unimportant though it may sound, when it happened to me it wasn't unimportant at all.

So, as I say, I gave it up. Every now and again I'm compelled to realize that I retain my gift as a sensitive, but I don't encourage it. I'm still insatiably curious about such things, still terribly fascinated, but the instant I feel the thing stirring inside me—prescience, precognition, any minor manifestation of that sort—I *shut* the door on it firmly. And gifts, did I call them? Impediments rather when you're situated as I am; you can't waste time on matters of that sort when you've got to make a living.

And now that I've told you the failures in my life, I'll tell you the success, the triumph, the lovely living important thing, which is my niece. I'm in danger of babbling on and on I fear, once started, but it makes me so happy just to think of her and talk about her. She's medium tall with the excellent shape proper to her time of life, swift clean proportions, with thick hair like a heavy cap, of an odd shade of brown, no lustre to it at all—what's called either matt brown or dead-leaf brown. But curiously, this lightless brown is the exactly right setting for her skin, very clear and luminous, a sort of gardenia or cream. This flawless skin she makes up with a faint touch of colour, though it adds little to her. She has pleasant regular features with unusual amber-brown eyes and over them such beautiful arching eyebrows, exactly symmetrical. And out of this face, not strictly beautiful, there looks such kindness and sweetness, so much intelligence and vitality and fun, that just to see her is a sort of nourishment. And not just to her doting auntie, I'll have you know; I've seen passers-by smile involuntarily at sight of her; the quality of her face is catching. Her voice and her laugh are delightful, just what you'd expect from—

Oh dear, sorry to go on and on like this, only I must *still* tell you about her; it's got so much to do with what came later.

Now the thing I've always found most compelling about her, is her sense of purpose. A shapeless floundering life is what I know too much about, but *she* didn't flounder; she knew her goal and went for it, and though she hasn't attained it yet, she's on her way and always has been. First she took a job with an interior decorator and learned all she could from him; he was knowledgeable apparently, though he seemed an undesirable type from my point of view—I hadn't met him then. After that she parted from him amicably and went to work for an antique dealer in rather an important way of business, and *slaved* at it, absolutely, and learned a lot more—yet never intended to stop in that job, good and interesting as it was. Her real ambition's to be a keeper in a museum, a specialist in fabrics, for which she has an absolute passion. During her holidays she'd go to France and Belgium, to where they've been famous for tapestries, historically famous for centuries, and learn about those giant looms and the various stitches—knottings?—and how to repair, clean and preserve them. And she was a pupil at Guilds of Needleworkers at home and abroad, and learned things like Elizabethan tent-stitch and Jacobean stump-work, all those curious dead skills you only see looking at you from inside glass cases. She's wonderful with her hands, of course; she can do anything with her hands.

Now that steady sense of purpose is something that rivets me with wonder and envy, when I contrast it with the fate of single women in my generation. If you failed to marry you were a failure in every other way, personal and social—Oh yes, in England it was still like that, quite up to World War Two; it's only in the last few decades that the useful but unskilled spinster is dying off as a social phenomenon. But *hordes* of us existed then, humble creatures willing to do almost anything for a home—usually with some relation, where we were put upon and reminded openly or silently of our dependence. . . . Well, too late for regret, too late.

Now a girl like Christabel, you'd expect to be living on her own. Or sharing a flat with another girl or even with a man; it's a commonplace thing nowadays. But the amazing thing is, she does nothing of the sort. She lives with *me,* and of her own free will. And why should she? I'm a leftover, I'm stupid and uninteresting; I'd be the last to blame her if she wanted her freedom. And even more remarkable than stopping with me, she does something else: *she admits me into her life.* That's a great thing, you must admit, considering the age-gap and other inequalities between us. But she ignores them, she tells me the day's doings and talks of holiday plans; we've had some lovely holidays together.

It's only on the subject of men—when she happens to discuss them—that her tone really troubles me. She's too critical and too flippant; too off-hand, as if she couldn't be bothered. Now that sort of thing may be all very well at eighteen or nineteen, but the years in which you can afford it aren't unlimited. She's young, yes, but one morning one can wake up to hear the drums of marching time no longer in brisk joyful staccato, but slower somehow, dragging . . . well, there's nothing I can do about it. Has she had affairs? I'd expect so, but I don't know. She runs her own life and is demonstrably more successful at doing it than I was, and I'd never presume to pry.

Her name by the way is Christabel Warne; her friends call her Chris but not I, I think Christabel's so pretty. My sister and her husband died in a pile-up on one of those horrible motorways—he at once and she in hospital a few hours later. So Christabel, at the age of six, had no family but me. And from the first I was furiously, utterly determined that if her life were going to be spoiled and thwarted, like mine, at least it shouldn't be for lack of a first-class education. All my energy and resolution went into that. There was some insurance, not much. You'd expect a fairly successful man to have protected his survivors more adequately; the fact remains that he hadn't done.

Oh, how I hoarded what money there was. Oh, what hours and what burning shoulder-blades at my sewing-machine—and in the end I triumphed. And it *was* a triumph, hers and mine, it was, it was. She showed a leaning toward arts at once, and went to excellent schools, then to LMH (as they call it), and you don't get into Lady Margaret Hall without the most stringent personal interview, let me tell you. And if I worked hard, my little girl worked harder. You see, she knew the situation. She knew because I'd explained how it was—that everything depended on herself. I hated to burden anything so small and young with responsibility for the future, but I had to. And even now I could cry, remembering those eyes fixed on me, that expression so pitiably anxious and serious, poor little thing. But she rose to it, how she rose to it, that gallant baby. 'A' levels most of the time and a First in

Arts and History at LMH—not that I was surprised. But you *see* how unfit I am to be the companion of such a girl. Was it a sense of duty that was keeping her with me?

I used to worry over that, oftener than you'd believe.

It all began after we'd had notice to vacate our flat. We'd fixed it up so nicely and comfortably, too; nowadays one hasn't a moment of security. A lease running out, a take-over, a big demolition scheme—there's always something to uproot you and turn you into a hunted creature trying to find a place for yourself and your bits and pieces, worried frantic all the time that you won't find it. Skyhigh London rents, unfurnished flats literally disappearing— well, I needn't tell you. But whereas we'd lived in Chelsea almost within sight of the river, now we were driven over the bridge to Battersea and Clapham. And with it, all the depression of having to hunt in so depressing a time of year—early February.

Now maybe you don't know Clapham and similar approaches to London. You can't, if your knowledge is limited to driving through the High Street, solidly lined with shops and *choked* with people and traffic. But turn off them just a little way and you'll find rows and rows of oldish houses quite undisturbed, seedy and out-of-date but often not hopelessly nor offensively so, not yet. But don't, I beg you, get the idea that accommodation is easily had in them, any more than in London. Everything's full to bursting, everything's been snatched up, the need is desperate—except that we hadn't realized, Christabel and I, exactly how desperate. She took a few days off on purpose and we tramped and slogged for miles, we confronted unpromising faces, we saw squalid holes at fantastic rents. And I leave you to imagine the misery of it, the desolation

16

of homelessness and fear in an elderly woman, if I'd had to do it alone. But I wasn't alone, by my side there marched a lovely young being with fine springy legs and springy optimism, and her mere presence held me up when I was so glassy-eyed with exhaustion I could hardly put one foot in front of the other.

Well, it was during one of my worst and groggiest spells that we found ourselves in this particular street. Not far outlying, even, but its character was peculiar; anything but residential, curiously silent and unpeopled, with shut-up brick buildings that looked like depots of one kind or another. There was a vast partially-excavated area with a construction company's sign in front, but nothing going on; all quiet and empty as if some project'd been postponed or abandoned. And between one of those sealed-up depots, and a mournful shop announcing RADIOS TELEVISION ACCESSORIES REPAIRS, was this house.

Literally, it was something to fetch a gasp out of you. It was painted all over in the vilest shade of chartreuse you ever saw, with its front door and window surrounds in an equally vile shade of mauve, an effect you can't imagine; it must have been done by some lunatic. We looked at each other with (I imagine) a simultaneous incredulity and burlesque of nausea. 'Enough to make one throw up—' Christabel began, then stopped. She'd caught sight of something, in fact at the same moment that I'd done; the madhouse colour-scheme'd distracted us, I expect. The monstrosity stood separated from its neighbours by strips of side-garden; it also had a patch of ground in front, behind the usual iron railings, and on one of the spikes was fastened a bit of paper.

'What's it say, do you suppose?' Christabel ventured. 'Let's go and see.'

'Someone's lost cat,' I moaned despondently.

'How do you know? They might have rooms or something.'

'In that *horror*? Even if they had, I'd never—'

'Oh, come on,' she urged. 'Let's not go home again with nothing at all accomplished. Come on,' she cajoled. 'No harm in looking.'

She started to cross the road, and perforce I had to come too. It was just at this instant—as I stepped off the kerb—that something hooked my innermost vitals like an iron talon, an . . . *agony* . . . of unwillingness? dread? I still don't know what; it was a lightning-stroke, instantly gone, yet the speed of it was so utterly incompatible with its force, its cruel *depth*. . . .

Then it'd vanished, no trace of it left at all, and then we stood before the row of iron palings. The notice attached to them was no bigger than a bit of writing-paper, just a square cut from a cardboard box apparently, a dark grey colour as if actually preferring to avoid notice—and on it were four words, block capitals in ink: ACCOMMODATION TO BE AVAILABLE. That way of putting it I found curious at once, very curious indeed. You'd expect something forthright, like ROOMS TO LET; instead, here was this wording which suggested to me a sort of cautiousness, like someone not wanting to commit himself (or herself, more probably) too far.

'Why don't we find out about this?' my niece was saying.

I opened my mouth to demur, then shut it. She was quite right; in our situation we couldn't afford to turn up our noses at any possibility. She was already pulling open the gate, and submissively I trailed her up the cracked flagstone walk, fifteen feet long at most, yet managing in its brevity the absurd flourish of a curve. And now that we were actually upon it, other things about the house surprised me. True that the colours were enough to scare you into fits, true that the patch of front garden had naked packed soil with a few starving straggles of privet-hedge, true that it was melancholy-looking; in this dreary silent street, on a grey February day, everything was melancholy. And yet, close to, the house wasn't derelict, which I'd expected it to be. The railings were a quite presentable black, the paintwork wasn't broken or peeling or blistering. Halfway above ground-level rose a basement window, unusually spacious; the windows and doors were generously proportioned. The place had had some care given it till recently, and at one time must have been a better class of house than at first appeared.

But also—just in those few seconds it'd taken to reach the nauseous mauve door—other things were happening to me. Beneath my submission to Christabel's decree that we must investigate the forlorn hope, beneath my vague leavings of opposition—and to my indescribable dismay—I felt the old enemy creeping upon me, the *otherness*. Oh! and by now I can tell you almost exactly what it's like. Most of us have had an anaesthetic at one time and another, I expect; well, this thing is identical with those first instants when you're beginning, just beginning, to go under. You're still awake, you're still you but you're being *enclosed* by something outside yourself, you're a candle that's dying, going out . . . yes, that's what it's like. And I've told you how I've blocked it off—successfully, most times, and like all disused faculties it tended to manifest itself rarely, and always more weakly. But this wasn't weak, it was flooding over me irresistibly, welling up and up; it had total hold of me as Christabel pressed the button within the heavy old-fashioned brass surround with its legend from bygone days, NO TRADESMEN, NO HAWKERS, its letters still faintly black. Yes, you're able to notice things like that, even in a state of possession. It's as though some part of you were still observing things, but remotely; unimportantly. And as the door was pulled open and a woman stood there, the otherness swam and mounted in my head to a climax like a wave breaking, and out of it my own voice spoke to her, loud yet silent: *I know you.* Needless to say, I'd never seen her before in all my life.

She was big and fairly tall, with heavy bones and plenty of weight on them, but her massiveness was well-controlled if sombre; her rather coarse dark hair with not much grey in it parted and drawn back, and her dark dress plain and substantial, what you could see of it under a heavy-duty apron. Her squared-off oblong face with its thick eyebrows, and her manner, were reserved to the point of being—I was going to say discouraging, but forbidding's more like it; that's the word, forbidding.

'Yes?' she said, her tone not exactly discourteous, but off-putting. It was Christabel who spoke up—I'd gone dumb as a fish—and asked, 'We were wondering if we might see the—the rooms?' Her polite voice had gone uncertain on the final word; you could tell she didn't know how to interpret that ambiguous ACCOMMODA-TION.

The woman hesitated. Not long, but perceptibly; besides the pause for the obvious purpose of looking the two of us over, she seemed to be involved in other considerations. But finally she said, 'Yes, I daresay it's all right.' The words I'd have taken to be grudging, but her air wasn't grudging—only noncommittal. She stood aside, and we stepped into a chilly tiled vestibule, after which she closed the street door and led us through double inner doors, their lower halves wood and upper ones stained glass, small panes in hideous shades of blue, green and mustard.

'It's on the first floor, just up those stairs,' she said, indicating. The hall was perfectly typical, quite wide, with a not-ungraceful flight of stairs going up along the left-hand wall; also on our left was a deep chimney recess with the old-fashioned hall stove still in it. Those stoves persisted till quite recently, I've seen them well into the sixties and beyond; beautiful objects when burnished by maids to velvet black rimmed with gleaming steel or brass, and still not unhandsome.

Sleepwalking always, silent always, I started to climb, with Christabel coming along behind me. The sense of otherness and recognition was ebbing; sometimes it disappears quickly and sometimes not. We were walking down the upper hall toward the front—the woman hadn't made the least offer to come with us—when Christabel, apparently judging that we were out of earshot, muttered, 'Odd, isn't it, that she never mentioned what sort of thing she had for rent, or where to go?' And enough was left, of my remoteness, for a very faint and receding voice to answer silently, *It's all right, I know where to go*. Aloud I said, 'Well, we'll soon see for ourselves,' and opened the door farthest front.

As soon as we'd passed through I'd come back to myself completely, and saw at once how foolish I'd been to go fancying that I knew the place—foolish because all houses of that period, 1820 to 1840 and built for ordinary comfortable middle-class people, are all alike. You know in advance there'll be a big kitchen in the basement with a servants' dining-room and various cubbyholes, including one with a marble shelf for meats. You know the ground floor'll be a big front room and a still bigger room in back looking out on the garden that existed at one time or still does exist. The first floor will have a big front room, the bedroom of master and mistress, and rear bedrooms of lesser degree. Bathrooms in houses of that type have certainly been put in much later, and those you find —if not recently modernized—are grim affairs. The second floor will have been the nursery and more bedrooms for the numerous Victorian offspring, and the third floor is servants' bedrooms and an attic. All of it a cut-and-dried pattern; no wonder I'd known what to expect, without dragging in second sight.

What I couldn't have foreseen, however, was the attractiveness of that front room—big, lofty, perfectly square, and even on this cheerless day surprisingly light. It had a handsome mantel with a blocked-off fireplace, and in the recess the customary stove of later date, this one unfortunately rusted to nothing. Of course it was all shabby and begrimed—but only with neglect, not with defilement of vandals' filth, like so many nowadays. This was mere ordinary dust and dirt; nothing about it that wouldn't yield to soap and water and fresh paint.

All this time we'd simply stood silent, turning slowly and staring about us. Finally Christabel opened the rather stately door midway of the rear wall, and we walked into a dark passage. Its entire left wall was drawers and cupboards, with a marble-topped basin in the middle; in the right wall were two doors. Inside the first was pitch-dark. We'd brought no torch, but Christabel snapped on her lighter and moved it about. A good-sized cubbyhole with some rotting shelves, cracked linoleum, a single electric point, broken; obviously the kitchen. There was a minute corner basin too, a horrible object.

'I'm sure all the wiring is dangerous,' my niece murmured, and I murmured back, 'Completely, I expect.'

'What's in here?' She was opening the second door and pitting her insufficient lighter against more Stygian blackness—of a bathroom. 'My God,' she said, which seemed adequate comment, and we moved toward the rear; the landlady'd given us no hint whatever that *Rooms* meant a self-contained flat comprising the whole first floor. Back here it was again very light for all the dull day, and divided into two quite decent bedrooms; each had its door opening independently into the bathroom-and-kitchen passage, a great amenity. We were more silent now, always moving more slowly, the way people do when absorbing new impressions that give rise to more and more active trains of thought. The rear windows showed a clean barren backyard, paved over, with a low wall at the end of it; beyond that loomed up another of those depot-looking places with a dead look about it. Not an inspiring view, but on the other hand not squalid; one could ignore it. Still wordless we turned to go back, moving—I realize now—with a sort of puppetlike unanimity, as if on a single string. We got into the front room again, and this time it looked bigger, brighter and of cleaner proportions than before.

'It could be made lovely.'

We said it together, at exactly the same moment. Then we burst out laughing, at exactly the same moment. We're always doing that, coming out in chorus with the same ideas, and whenever it happens it gives me the same ridiculous pleasure.

'Oh Christabel.' I was quivering all over. 'Let's go talk to her quickly, quickly—'

'Hold it, darling,' she interrupted. You see how our roles were reversed all at once; now it was she who was holding me back and I that'd gone to the other extreme, longing to plunge in blindly—a classic trait of weak characters, I've heard.

'We don't even know how she wants to rent it,' continued my niece, 'or what she expects for it. Let her put in a few sticks of furniture and pack in four girls at five pounds a head—at least—and she can get twenty pounds a week without quivering an eyelash. And she knows she can get twenty or more—she must know.'

While I listened, progressively silent—

'We can't begin to pay twenty a week,' she was saying. 'Or anything like it.'

'I expect you're right,' I murmured after a moment; the heart'd gone out of me at once. Over-enthusiastic or over-dejected, always going to extremes, like the fool I am. And been reminded often enough how much of a fool, and unsparingly too, I promise you. So I pursued dolefully, trying to comfort myself, 'Anyway, I expect transport'd be impossible for you—getting back and forth to work.'

'Transport's all right,' she said at once. 'I saw the good old 137 bus pass the bottom of the road—over the bridge and right into Sloane Street, like a bird.'

'Oh!' Her antique shop is in Sloane Street. 'Yes, that's so.—Oh darling, couldn't we just talk to her, just find out the lay of the—'

'Wait, wait,' she restrained me; I was champing at the bit all over again. 'I don't expect anyone'll snap it up, not all that quickly. Just let me think.' She cogitated, while I fretted. 'I'll bet you anything that the wiring *is* gone, com-

24

pletely. And there's no heating, of course. And it needs drastic cleaning and redecorating, and I promise you *she* won't do anything about it—we'll have to do it all ourselves. So in the first place—if she'd let us have it—we'd have to spend the earth fixing it up.'

'Yes, but moving anywhere would cost the earth. And we could do such a lot, ourselves—the place is worth it.'

'Yes, that's so.—I wonder,' she digressed, 'if there's hot water—?' She disappeared into the passage, and reappeared. 'Yes, it came up a bit rusty but quite hot. I'd half expected the pipes would've packed up.'

'Oh Christabel,' I burst out. 'Do let's talk to her.'

'All right, let's,' she said, and with her agreement I felt the courage running out of me straightaway; a fool, and a cowardly fool.

'You talk to her,' I petitioned.

'No, you.'

'Oh dear,' I waffled abjectly.

'I saw how you disliked her at sight,' Christabel pursued. 'Even just standing there in the doorway she seemed to put you off—just knock the words right out of you.'

She was so far from knowing the truth that she'd taken my instinctive recoil, there on the front steps, for mere dislike. She knows nothing whatever about these curious extra faculties of mine; my secrecy in regard to them, I've often heard, is very common among people with *genuine* para-normal endowment. I'll come to that in its place. But remember, always remember that these unprofitable gifts of mine were unknown to my niece, unknown *completely*.

'I'll be there alongside of you,' she was encouraging meanwhile. 'If you overlook a point I'll mention it, and you'll do the same when I forget. But *you* must take charge—you're head of the family.'

Head of the family! You see how she upholds the weak reed, how she protects my dignity? Is it any wonder that I adore her?

'But let's be cautious, Lorna, let's not show her we're all that keen. Above all,' she exhorted, 'let's find out how long her leasehold's got to run. If she only has this house for three or four years more, it's no use.'

A good thing too, that she'd mentioned the lease; I was so scatty with excitement, and the necessity of not showing it, that I might have forgotten this all-important point— along with God knows how many others.

So the two of us went down together.

The woman reappeared from the far end of the hall as we reached the bottom of the stairs. She came toward us without haste, and again her manner extended and rein- forced the odd little notice outside—no visible anxiety nor even interest in our reaction or decision, nothing but that same air of being unready to commit herself to anything, one way or the other.

'We've—we've looked at the rooms.' However haltingly, I was obliged to speak first; obviously she wasn't going to. 'And we wondered if we might have a word with you, Mrs. . . . ?'

She hesitated—only the fraction of an instant, but per- ceptibly—before opening a door on her left. 'In here, we'd better,' she motioned, and we filed in ahead of her and took seats at her second gesture. This room was the twin of the one above it, a lofty square, not quite as light as the other. It was completely furnished and in rigid order— a carpet, a three-piece suite and additional chairs, a glass-fronted cupboard, a clock and some ornaments on the mantelpiece, sheer curtains and brocade overdrapes at the window. Everything little-used and clean, yes, but the whole effect dead and comfortless, with that mass-produced poverty of taste that made you cringe; the colours muddy yet managing to clash, the fine mantelpiece disfigured by some trashy gewgaws scattered along it. Christabel, I knew, must have taken in the mediocrity of it more thoroughly than I could ever do, but of course she just sat primly, not saying anything. And now that I could see the woman in a better light, upright and impassive, with a look of sitting in judgment—a sort of pompousness—I felt again that curious stirring of familiarity, only this wasn't the moment for thinking about it.

'This is my niece, Miss Warne,' I essayed, still awkwardly. 'And I am Miss Teasdale.'

'Mrs. Rumbold,' the graven image vouchsafed—just that much and no more.

'Well, we've looked at the rooms, as I've said,' I pursued. 'But we wondered how you were wishing to let them, as separate rooms or as—'

'As a flat,' she interrupted at once; I was surprised to get that much show of decision out of her. 'I couldn't consider letting them as separate rooms.'

'Well, that would suit us very well,' I offered cautiously. 'We'd be interested in it as a flat.'

Again she was silent, and again I was more struck by her appearance in detail, the sallow skin, the unrevealing dark eyes with heavily-marked eyebrows, the lowering, forbidding look; anachronistic like a daguerreotype, or a menacing Dickens character. And yet with her silence, her manner had changed very subtly; she seemed more willing to listen, even to listen with the beginnings of interest.

'Only, would you please tell us,' I plowed on, 'how long is your lease? Because, if it runs out in a couple of years or so—'

'It's freehold,' she interrupted again. 'It's our house.' (*Our:* a husband?)

'Well.' I wanted to exchange glances with Christabel, but refrained. 'Well, in that case—'

Not a word from the creature, I'd never seen anything like it; she was obviously determined that I should do all the talking.

'You see, anything we took would have to be on a long lease,' I laboured on. 'We'd hope to settle in for a good while and improve the place very much, and naturally we shouldn't wish to have all that work and expense and then be obliged to move—'

'I'd want a long let,' she cut across me in her unattractive voice—not uneducated exactly, only by fits and starts. Still, her words held the first hint of positiveness we'd extorted from her, so far; I was about to continue when Christabel asked in a soft undemanding voice, 'Would there be hot water?'

'Oh yes, I've put in a storage system. Not for heating,' she added hastily. 'It just heats our part, the basement and ground floor only. But there's good hot water always, it's thermostatic.'

'Hot water's *so* important,' my niece said shyly, like an ingenue. 'Now it seemed to us that the electric wiring wasn't in very good condition, and there're hardly any points—?'

'The wiring ain't—isn't bad,' Mrs. Rumbold said with a first faint aggressiveness. 'It's all right.'

'But supposing you accepted us as tenants,' Christabel continued gently. 'Since you say there's no heating—?'

'No heating.'

'Well, we'd have to have Dimplex or something, wouldn't we, and one needs high power points for those. Would you object if we rewired the whole flat?'

'No, I shouldn't object,' the woman returned promptly for once, and I thought, *No, I should think not*. She'd put my back up obscurely but definitely. *Why should you object to people spending a hundred and fifty at least on rewiring your property*, I pursued my unfriendly reflections, *to say nothing of paint and repairs and so forth?*

'Well.' I'd had to resume, with spurious amiability. 'Would you care to discuss terms now, or would you—'

'Well, not straightaway.' She'd a habit of breaking in when people spoke; in addition to her *manner*, which wasn't pleasant, her manners weren't good. 'I'd have to speak to my daughter first.'

'Oh, I see.' (*We* not a husband, apparently, but a daughter.)

'If my daughter were at home we could talk it over soon as you like,' she continued. 'But she's never home this time of day, she goes to business.'

A bit of refainment I've always detested; why not say she goes to work? And above and beyond that, and only when she'd repeated the word *daughter*, did her curious inflection on it come home to me—a dignity in it, almost a reverence, as if invoking some power far above us. At once, however, my first amusement gave way to understanding. She was *proud* of her daughter, that was all; proud with a pride so intense it seemed to inflate her, for the moment, pneumatically.

'But I could talk to her this evening,' she pursued. 'So if you ladies'd like to come back tomorrow . . .'

She was so perfectly indifferent it annoyed me all over again. Annoyed or not, however, there it was, take it or leave it.

We made an appointment for the day following, and went.

Naturally we talked of nothing else for the rest of the day and far into the evening, going at it hammer and tongs, pros and cons, veering now this way and now that, and not—I must say—very consistently.

'I don't like her very much,' Christabel argued.

'Neither do I, and that's all to the good,' I argued back. 'A landlady that's friendly is dangerous, you're sure to fall out with her sooner or later, and then you've had it. The sort of unfriendliness that follows friendliness is the worst kind, always.'

'Welll—'

'This woman'll keep her distance, unless I'm much mistaken.'

'Oh yes, she's sure to. It's certainly a point.'

'But it *is* an enormous undertaking, doing the place over.' Now it was I who was sagging morally, in dubiousness and gloom. 'We'll have to put in all new bathroom fittings. *She* won't, depend upon it.' I gnawed a thumbnail. 'I hadn't counted on our spending that kind of money.'

'It's not so much, after all,' my girl gainsaid. 'If a few hundreds get us a settled home, it's a bargain.'

'Ye-es, that's so.'

'On the other hand, it's a fearful lot of work. The

cleaning alone—' Christabel stared at the rough prospect. 'No one's lived in those rooms for years, I expect.'

'All right. Shall I see if she's on the phone? Ring her and cancel the appointment?'

'Well, if you say.'

'Darling, *you* say.'

'Why I more than you? But all right, ring her then and say we're not coming.'

'Now wait, wait.' I'd one of those awful qualms—that panicky fear of doing the wrong thing. 'I mean, let's not be precipitate.'

'No, perhaps we shouldn't be.'

It was restful to have arrived at one point of agreement, anyway.

'The place,' Christabel ruminated, 'has such *possibilities.*'

Two points of agreement; we were making progress.

'I've spoken to my *daughter.*' Again that magisterial nuance, as to some high and mighty and final authority. Again we sat in that soul-destroying living-room, Christabel and I side by side and Mrs. Rumbold facing us. A little pale February sun straggled timidly along the carpet and emphasized the tastelessness of everything, the sterile pretentiousness.

'You see, this is the way of it.'

From the moment of our arrival she'd been perceptibly more discursive than yesterday, with far less abruptness and reserve.

'We own the house, as I've told you,' she was saying. 'Now of course we could split it up into cubbyholes and rent every one of them tomorrow, but you know what types'll take that sort of accommodation—the kind that'd wreck Bucknum Palace overnight, that kind would.'

We nodded cordial agreement.

'We don't want our house turned into a slum,' she pursued. 'And I'm alone all day, I can't cope with scum like hippies and junkies and that. And no matter what nasty filthy things they do to your property, you can't get them out. It means spending half your life before the Rent Tribunal—and have them decide against you, more likely than not. Landlords nowadays, you know, they haven't a hope.'

We agreed even more cordially.

'So all along my daughter's said to me, We'll be choosey. We'll wait for someone that wants a flat, people of the right type.'

We indicated a modest if silent hope that we *were* people of the right type.

'The little sign outside,' she pursued. 'Maybe you noticed how we'd put it? We didn't say we *had* accommodation, on'y that we *might* have. Come right out with it and say you've got rooms, you've got to let 'em in or risk a fine. But say you *may* be having 'em, and they can't hold you to anything. She—my *daughter*—she thought it out.' She bridled complacently. 'The way we'd say it.'

'Very clever,' I blandished like a sycophant.

'So we talked it over.' She was well launched now; the admiration we'd provided certainly hadn't done us any harm. 'And we thought, seeing you ladies would want the whole first floor as a unit, one flat—?'

'Yes,' I said as she paused. 'As one flat.'

'And for living purposes only? No business?'

'Certainly not.' This was startled out of me before I'd

32

thought; her question had caught me on one foot. 'Just for residential purposes, of course.'

'And you're ready to improve the place—' her look and voice turned sly '—to landlord's advantage?'

'Well.' I'd been taken aback by the dimension of her greed; one glimpse had been enough. 'Within reason, of course.'

'We're not millionaires,' Christabel put in disarmingly.

'Well, you gave me the impression you'd want to improve it,' shrugged the woman. 'I can rent it tomorrow, as is.'

'But doesn't that mean,' Christabel queried innocently, 'letting in exactly the type of tenant you don't want?'

As this impaled the woman on a momentary quiet—

'And by the way, supposing we lived here,' my young warrior turned on the enemy camp, 'is it quiet here? Because quiet's very important to my aunt and me—'

'Oh, it's quiet all right,' the other interrupted. 'Just like it is now. And no one living over you—I shan't be doing up the second floor for a while yet. So you'd be quiet, all right. I like a quiet house myself.'

From there on we began discussing practical terms of tenancy, and at once it was ding-dong ding-dong all the way—with Christabel bearing the brunt; I'd known she'd have to, in the end. The woman would concede nothing and repair nothing, and we had to give way on all counts. The rent wasn't low God knows, but we'd have had to pay a third as much again in Kensington or Chelsea or even Fulham, we knew that. So did Mrs. Rumbold, I promise you. Then came the question of what she'd called a 'long let', and here Christabel and I stood shoulder to shoulder—there had to be a lease. She didn't like that; people of her class hate firm agreements, they want something they can wriggle out of. But here we wouldn't yield and she had to agree in the end, grudgingly; all the same it was we who had to find a solicitor—and pay the fees, naturally. When at last everything was settled we were utterly worn out with meeting, and overcoming, the woman's obstructiveness and ever-ready suspicions, so typical of the half-educated. On the other hand Mrs. Rumbold—stimulated no doubt by the cheque of deposit, and by the thought of tenants about to spend several hundred pounds in improving her property—waxed talkative all at once.

'A house can be an awful burden,' she confided gloomily. 'The second floor still to do, and on top of that the attic and a lot o' nasty little cubbyholes. That attic,' she sighed. 'I dread the thought of it. Solid with muck it is, just solid.'

'There're people that clear out junk and take it away,' Christabel suggested. 'If you rang one of those—'

'Before I've looked it over myself?' she broke in aggressively. 'With all that stuff you see in the papers about antiques and val'able paintings being found in places like that? I'll go through every inch of it before I let anything out of *this* house, you bet.'

'You're quite right,' I murmured.

'But I don't feel up to it, not yet. Fixing up the place so nice, just these two floors where we live, it's taken it out of me. The work, you won't believe—getting it the way you see it.' Her tone was condescending, her glance at the room proprietary and complacent; Christabel and I avoided looking at each other.

'What does she think she'll find in the attic?' my niece conjectured on the way home. 'Original Rembrandts?'

She was silent a moment. 'Her soul's exactly like her living-room, did you notice?'

I'd been thinking that myself, in more or less the same words.

So that February and March, oh dear, I don't want to live through anything like *that* again. Going by bus between Chelsea and Clapham in the wretched weather—both months exceptionally cold and rainy—always reaching home in a state of collapse and having to drag myself out next morning all over again: still, no help for it. Christabel'd already taken time off for hunting and had to get back to her job; someone had to mount guard in the flat and keep an eye on things generally, seeing what the British workman's up to nowadays in the way of muddle and mess, completely without conscience.

First though the two of us'd worked like ditch-diggers—swept the whole place out three times, ripped out decayed shelving and rotten linoleum and pulled out rusty nails by the hundred; when we'd got through the decks were cleared for action, bare as the back of your hand. By the way, my niece had taken the lease downstairs—signed with my name and the proper form of hers, Mortimer-Warne, though she never uses it except for documents like this one and rather laughs at it—and it turned out that the daughter had opened the door and accepted it. 'What's she like?' I asked idly, and Christabel said, 'Gracious but reserved, *very* good-looking. They've decided we're a bit below their standard, obviously,' and I smiled and said, 'All to the good.'

We'd taxied a couple of chairs over to our new domain, and a carton with cups and saucers and biscuits. There was no current—rewiring was going on first thing, of course—so I'd lug a thermos along. And there I'd sit turning blue with cold day after day, making sure the electricians didn't put the power points in all the wrong places, just for fun. After the electricians, came the plumbers. I watched as they staggered out under the old bath huge as a sarcophagus with its enamel eaten away down to the iron, and uprooted other grisly relics about which the less said the better. We were putting in modern fitments mostly at our expense; the landlady'd stood to it that the bath and the cracked basin were 'all right', though she agreed to pay half for the 'toilet', as she called it; wouldn't you know. Naturally she'd meant the very cheapest type of thing, so what she coughed up in the end amounted to a quarter of the cost, not half. We didn't mind that so much, though; we expected to live with those things for a long time.

I'm not forgetting, either, what had hung over me since the day we'd definitely taken the flat, and which I'd begun by keeping to myself. But it got to be too much for me, too heavy, and finally—

'I'm worried about that lie I told her,' out I came with it. 'I was afraid she wouldn't let us have it, I expect, if she knew I was a working seamstress. But if she latches onto it—from customers coming and going—she might just choose to make trouble, say we'd violated the terms of the lease or God knows what.'

'But you're *not* a seamstress,' my girl contradicted airily. 'You've stopped being one, didn't you know?'

'No, I did *not* know,' I said coldly. 'All I know is that we've both had to work, always, to keep any place going. And where's this one different? A fine thing if we spent the earth fixing up the woman's mouldy old barrack, and then gave her grounds for slinging us out.'

'Shut up, darling, will you? and listen? Ron Dancey's dying to have you.'

Ronald Dancey was her first employer—the decorator she'd worked for, before going on to Alec Sterrett's antique business.

'He's panting for you,' she continued, and I said, 'I thought he was angry with you for leaving?'

'That was only for a while, he's simmered down now. We've always kept in touch, we're quite good friends.'

'Oh.'

'And he's got an old faithful who's been doing his curtains for years and years, and now she's retiring. And Ron's going mad, of course—climbing every wall in sight.'

She was deliciously smug and superior as she saw me catching on.

'So hey presto, plain seamstress into decorator's assistant,' she announced. 'Anyway you'll have to be mounting guard at the flat till the workmen are out, so you'd have to let your customers go in any case.'

'Welll . . .'

'And after we've settled in, you'll need a long rest. *And,*' she announced pugnaciously, 'I'm going to see that you get it. And when you're well and truly rested and not before, you'll do curtains for Ron.'

'But—' I looked as vacant as I sounded, no doubt; being rushed always bewilders me. 'How do you know that my work can meet Ron's standards—'

'Oh darling, don't be silly,' she jumped on me. 'Curtains are more straightforward than lumps and bumps and alterations, aren't they? To say nothing of the fact that the work isn't all that steady—not heavy enough to attract attention? And about the fancy bits like pelmets and swags and tie-backs, Ron's old girl will instruct you first. He does things the right way, old Ron the fairy—the stain-less-steel fairy.'

'Well . . .'

'Poor darling, I've rather bulldozed you with it, haven't I?' She was amused and indulgent. 'But once you get used to the idea, you see how good it is, don't you? How practical?'

'Well.' Another of those feeble *wells*, as if they were all I could contribute. But already I was entering into the idea, and for such a habit-bound creature as myself, rapidly. I've already told you that our chief support—when Christabel was a little girl—was my work as a plain dress-maker. And in those days there was no lack of them, and you hung onto your customers for all you were worth, I promise you. You flattered and kow-towed and submitted to their exactions, anything not to lose them. Of course when Christabel began working, and the money was better, and the plain seamstress a commodity already dis-appearing off the face of the earth, things became a little easier. For instance, a favourite trick of some women was to bring you—with that odious combination of blandishment and cunning—a piece of material that wasn't *quite* suf-ficient, and ask you to get two blouses out of what was enough for one blouse and seven-eighths. And the better-off the woman was, the more apt she'd be to play those penny-pinching tricks. And in the old days I had to go along with her, I'd make pattern after pattern and rack my brains and get nervous headaches trying to do the impossible—which I managed to do, most times, so that some rich harpy could brag to her friends how cleverly she'd wormed extra value out of me. And you won't be-lieve the *pleasure* it gave me, the first time I could afford to look a woman in the eye and say coldly, 'No, Mrs. Blank,

38

the piece isn't big enough, and I shouldn't care to put so much effort into it.' Oh, that moment—pure bliss. And now, in the wink of an eye, my girl was transforming me from a drudge into something quite different, my Christabel was doing that for me. She'd been watching as I kindled to the idea, slowly, for she said triumphantly, 'Aha!' She can always do that with me—follow my thinking—and so to a lesser degree can I with her.

'It'll fascinate you,' she was saying. 'Some of the materials are simply breath-taking.'

'And you say you're sure there's not a—' I quavered a bit '—a great deal of work to handle?'

'In my experience of him, no. He's got a little specialty, sort of—beautiful single windows for art galleries, expensive restaurants, places like that. It's interesting to do, and not rushed—rather off and on, even rather slow at times. And doing that sort of work—' she sounded completely confident '—there's a thousand less chances of attracting the woman's notice than if you went back to dressmaking.'

'You think so . . . ?'

'I *do*. Also this way you've plenty of time to get rested, because his curtain expert isn't retiring for another three months.'

'I should be working sooner than that,' I whimpered. 'The *money* we've spent—!'

'Don't worry, Lorna.' She was peremptory. 'We'll be all right, you'll see.'

So there it rested.

On a morning of cold and rain, with plenty of wind to whip the rain horizontally, I was occupying my perch in the front room of the flat. At the other end the workmen were making their accustomed row—banging, whistling, far too much conversation—and already I was properly frozen, though it was barely noon. The chill in those rooms was lethal, a saved-up chill of all those unheated past winters; the tea from my thermos had been thermos-hot, not really hot. So there I sat with hands and feet from which all sensation had long departed, plus occasional shivering fits, when there came a tap at the half-open door, followed by Mrs. Rumbold's putting her head around it.

'Good morning, Miss Teasdale,' she said, with a contortion of the face obviously meant for a smile. 'I was wondering, could you do with a nice hot cuppa?'

'Good morning,' I returned. 'Why, that's very nice of you.' Out of total unpreparedness for such attentions from such a quarter I'd gone hesitant, thinking vaguely that perhaps our cheques of deposit and rent lay a bit heavy on her conscience—as if *her* conscience would protest at taking money for an uninhabitable flat. Above all though I was too cold to think quickly, my wits were too numbed to come up with a diplomatic refusal. So before I could think I heard myself repeating, 'That's really most kind of you.'

'My, it *is* perishing up here.' She'd come into the room. 'Do you good to come down and have a bit of a warm-up.'

'Or—on second thought—' I was floundering in retreat, too late '—perhaps I'd better be on the spot, the work-men—'

'It's almost noon, they'll be knocking off any minute now. Never slow about doing *that*, they aren't.' Already she was walking out of the room, taking it for granted that I'd follow. Which I did perforce, with belated consternation at having let myself be trapped. I didn't want her tea, I didn't want her warm-up, yet here I was, accepting favours from her—favours which in due course I'd be bound to reciprocate, in one way or another. Thanks to my failed presence of mind I was doing what we'd resolved not to do—have any relationship with the downstairs household, apart from ordinary business civility. Oh my thick stupid head, I could have kicked myself . . .

And yet during our descent, literally between one step and the next—marvellous how the mind works, isn't it—my attitude was transformed from reluctance to eagerness. For all Christabel's certainty that my making curtains wouldn't attract undue attention, it still worried me that the sounds of such industry might invite notice and (who knew) objections. How persistent this worry was, how nagging, I hadn't actually realized till it rushed out of hiding in this moment. But again in this moment, miraculously, I realized my luck and my opportunity—to learn the layout of the Rumbold flat, and from this knowledge learn where to place my sewing-machine.

So with sudden feverish alacrity, as I've said, I followed our landlady's massive rear down two flights and into the warmth of her kitchen. We had tea and she regaled me meanwhile with their own dire experiences of carpenters, electricians and plumbers, and of course I listened with utmost sympathy, with the inevitable result.

'I expect you'd like to see our flat,' she offered magnanimously, and of course I accepted with appropriate gratitude. Of our sightseeing tour I'll only say that everywhere was the same evidence of the mass-produced soul with its sterile comfortless environment; not a book in sight anywhere, God knows what they read—women's magazines and television news, I expect.

All the same, when I'd got back to my Siberia, I felt rich. I had my information—so invaluable, so essential.

41

Both Rumbold bedrooms were directly under our bedrooms, in the rear—I've said the floors were replicas of each other. The daughter's room had been instantly distinguishable with its dressing-table loaded with cosmetics and its lot of fussy little cushions on the bed. So at once I could see that the one and only place for my machine was in my bedroom, which I'd choose to have over the daughter's. She'd be out of the house by 9.30 at the latest I judged, though I'd have to do a little spying on that point; the mother—a house-proud woman if I ever saw one—would have tidied this holy of holies certainly by 10.30, however adoringly she lingered over it. And I'm not criticizing her; aren't I exactly the same way about Christabel? All I mean is, that the room beneath mine would be unoccupied, completely unoccupied, say between eleven (playing safe) and five. And if I couldn't get in a good solid four hours of work between those times, it would be very sad indeed.

So there I was, with that worrying hurdle got over. And how *glad* I was that I'd kept the problem of the machine from Christabel; she was carrying enough burdens without mine. Now I felt safe, safe and confident there could be no risk of my industry's annoying anyone, or indeed of its being noticed at all.

What a blessing to have that point settled once and for all; what a weight off my mind.

Well, I'll spare you the saga of our redecoration, except to say that it went faster than I could have believed. One hears hair-raising tales from people who've tried to improve a flat or even one room—tales of shoddy work, delays, excuses, carelessness—but we were lucky. And our luck was no accident, it was *created*, and by whom do you think? Oh she's so clever, that girl, and her decorator's experience'd given her so many contacts in all sorts of trades, and everyone obviously wanting to oblige her, and I don't wonder. In no time at all she'd men with terrifying high steps in and out of the flat, the ceilings beautifully done, and at professional rates. The walls and baseboards we painted ourselves, after the colour-scheme that she'd planned; the spacious living-room, especially, woke up from its long shabby sleep, so anxious to co-operate with us and be lovely again that it was touching. She *slaved*, literally, since all this had to be done after working hours. Toward eleven at night she'd be flat with exhaustion, all but prostrated, yet never cross or snappish with it, never; she was in such a glow at seeing how it was turning out that once in a while she'd fly at me and hug me, out of sheer excitement. Even dressed in a battered old shirt and jeans, and with that smudged look of overwork and fatigue upon her, I've never seen her prettier or so illumined with vitality. And finally she'd bought up at auction two big lots of fine thick Wilton, a beautiful shade of amber, and got *that* laid by a man employed by a big carpet firm, who did evening work on his own time—for a song, compared to the scandalous rates we'd have paid in the ordinary way. So there we were, with a *home*— permanent, or as permanent as one can say nowadays.

By the way, a small fleeting thing happened about then, which I'd better mention. It was Christabel's free afternoon and we were slogging away at the new flat, naturally. She was perched aloft wielding a paint brush, when all at once she glanced out of the window and the brush stopped dead in mid-stroke.

'She's going out—Ma Rumbold,' she said, scrambling off the ladder. 'Come on.'

'Where?'

'I want to see what's overhead.' She was making for the door. 'Come on, Lorna.'

'But why?'

'Didn't it strike you as peculiar, her saying she'd no intention of fixing the second floor for a long time yet? But wouldn't she need badly to fix it up for renting, toward the rates and whatnot of a big place like this? So what's wrong with it? What's the mystery?'

'But—'

'I just want an idea and I don't like mysteries. It won't take two minutes, we'll hurry. Come *on!*'

So—reprehensibly—the two of us scrambled upstairs. The silent dusty hall was narrower than ours; we skimmed up and down opening the five doors that led off of it. At the first one Christabel said under her breath, 'Oh Lord.' The other rooms called for no further amplification, and we got downstairs again without loss of time.

'No wonder,' she said when we'd got the door shut. 'A thousand pounds wouldn't begin to see her past that. Just a bathroom alone, she'd have to put one in—four or five hundred at least. No mystery, just a staggering expense for a woman like that—even borrowing, she'd have to go in pretty deep.'

She was right; no mystery whatever behind those five doors, only an indecent ruinousness such as our flat, in its worst days, couldn't have begun to match. Because those foetid dens couldn't have been anything but bedrooms, their walls long corrupt with the special exhalations of bedrooms; exhalation of sleep with windows closed, exhalation of sickness, of commodes, of pungent medicines and of steam from tin baths before open coal fires. And, as well, exhalations of dying; in houses over a century old people are bound to have died, who knows how many? It was all this cumulative onslaught, tainted with the body's fierce subtle acids (grisly thing the body, come to think) that had brought the paper peeling off the walls and ceilings in great soft flaps and stalactites, and left a deep necrotic smell that cut your breath. Small wonder that Mrs. Rumbold hadn't felt up to tackling it, not yet. . . .

'By the way.' My niece, swarming up to her perch, stopped again. 'Doesn't it strike you as odd that a woman like Mrs. Rumbold could have bought this place, *bought* it, mind you? You remember her telling us it was freehold?'

'Yes, I remember.'

'She'd have needed thousands, even for a wreck like this,' Christabel argued. 'Nothing's cheap any more. Where'd she get that kind of money?'

'Well, she might have inherited some, people do. And then, with a mortgage—'

'Yes, that must be it. All the same, I've rather a funny feeling.' But she spoke casually, half-dismissing the matter.

For myself, I'd no need to dismiss it; the point hadn't occurred to me as being interesting or important.

The tray sat on a low table between us. Not between Christabel and me, only between me and Mrs. Rumbold. This was my return—compulsory—for my visit to her flat. Both the visit, and this present occasion, remained my secret from my niece. And yet, if she'd blamed my mismanagement, what else could I have done? The time of day and the workmen knocking off had conspired to rob me of all excuse for sticking alone in that icy comfortless flat. Refusal of her blasted cup of tea, in those circumstances, would have exposed my desire of avoidance so glaringly that even she—thick-skinned as I judged her—couldn't have missed it.

But to tell you the truth, something new was dictating my actions, a feeling so strong it amounted to duress—that at all costs I musn't offend the woman. This may or may not have been part of my first response to the sight of her, that confused dreamlike shock of familiarity. I can't swear to the connection, I can only swear to my sudden knowledge—my *absolute* knowledge—of a darkness in her nature that I mustn't stir up, however far it took me out of my way. The precise geography of this Rumbold murk I couldn't make out, except for my certainty that it was there. And none of this was snobbery, I'll swear; who am I, a failure, to feel snobbish toward anyone? It was simply this vague inexplicable . . . *dread,* no less—of incurring her hostility. Call it cowardice, you'd be quite right, and like a coward I'd put my return invitation off and off. But the moment comes, inevitably, when you're nailed. Also the thought of her as the first guest in our home gave me no pleasure whatever, I promise you.

So here we sat, having tea in our living-room. The day was cheerless, but even by the unfavourable light you couldn't miss the triumphant success we'd achieved. She'd stopped short on crossing the threshold—stopped dead—for just that fraction of a moment. Devoid of taste as she was, all the same she'd realized what a fool she'd made of herself in showing me her hideous blighting flat with such complacence. And she didn't like it, she didn't like it a little bit; that was evident straightaway. The tea-tray also came under her instant disfavour as parading our possessions and showing her hospitality in an inferior light by contrast. All this you could see smouldering inside her—

see it by her sulky silence from the moment we sat down, by her eyes that never stopped moving in every direction, excluding none; I'd the awareness not only of her jealousy and resentment that she was controlling with an effort, but that it was bound to break out soon, in one form or another. And that I was secretly amused at her, for the moment, is only additional proof of what a fool I am.

'Well, it's a change,' was her first extended remark, over a second cup. 'It's certainly a change.'

'I hope you approve of it,' I smarmed too lyrically. 'We'd *like* you to approve, seeing that it's your house.'

The reminder of her proprietorship could be seen to mollify her. Only slightly though, and not nearly enough.

'Well yes, it's quite nice,' she grudged, her eyes travelling downward. 'That's very good carpet, your wall-to-wall.'

'We got it cheaply at auction,' I disclaimed. 'It was a great bargain.'

'Well, luck's better than brains they say,' was her graceful comment. 'I'd hate to pay out what you must have done for this painting job.'

'We did it ourselves,' I countered. 'All but the ceilings.'

'Oh.' Blocked in that direction, she found another. 'I daresay those window curtains cost you a pretty penny.'

'I made them myself.' It was true, also seeing a chance to plant the idea of sewing-machine activity, I grabbed it. 'They're from our old flat actually, I'll be making others as soon as we can afford the material. You've noticed already, of course, they're too short for these windows.'

She didn't answer; too busy ferreting out material for more offensive remarks. A rapid canvass of the furniture gave her what she needed.

'Well, it's not hard to do up a place all la-de-da,' she sniffed, 'when you've plenty of posh furniture.'

'Mahogany *is* old-fashioned, isn't it? And I'm afraid a good bit of it needs reupholstering,' I deprecated. 'Most of it belongs to my niece, actually—by inheritance.'

Now there, straightaway, was another odd thing. Even while I was preparing the tea-tray I'd somehow resolved absolutely that Christabel shouldn't appear in my conversation, not with *that* woman; I wouldn't refer to her be it ever so casually, I wouldn't even call her by name—and now I'd gone and done it. I can't explain, either, why my slip had given me such a sense of foreboding, as if in mentioning her name I'd . . . somehow . . . *exposed* her to something.

'That stuff too, it'd be from her people?' Her glance of naked assessment was now raking the mantelpiece, making the brave show its strong simple lines deserved—after how many tawdry dusty years, I wonder. Four framed samplers hung in a line above it, dim mellow old things, and between them stood a handsome old domed clock with a shining brass face. A few bits of silver, not valuable but pretty and well-polished, were ranged on either side.

'She's young to be an orphan,' the woman continued ferreting.

'Yes,' I said. 'Tell me, do you know anything of the history of this house?'

She paused, not only as if taken aback at the rudeness and abruptness of my digression, but as if making up her mind whether to resent it or not. And with this indecision something else, a discomfort? reluctance . . . ?

'About who built it, or anything?' I pursued. 'Or who lived in it last?'

'Well, I don't know.' Pause. 'They say one old lady lived

here till about 1930, just the one old lady alone. Or I *think* that's the story.' Her slow response confirmed to me not only her unwillingness but reserve, a sort of careful picking and choosing. 'Eighty-five or more she was, I think someone told me—but who or when or where, I can't recall.' She paused again. 'Or that's how I remember it.'

'I see.' I was interested; not in her old lady especially. Far too often one reads of these pathetic hermits found dying or dead in their solitudes, and then only because the milk bottles've piled up for several days. No, what continued to intrigue me was her cautiousness of manner —unless I was imagining things. 'And after this old lady what happened? Would you know?'

'Well, as I understand, some kin of hers got it, some middle-aged couple, and lived here from 'bout 1930.' It still came out of her rather reluctantly. 'She outlived him— she's dead no more'n a couple of years ago, I think.'

'The last of the family died as recently as 1970?' I'd found a bit of Victoriana to sink my teeth into. 'This place was built about 1840, by the look of it. So if the last in-heritor's just only died, it means that one family've had it for well over a century. Would you know their name?'

'How would I know?' she repudiated with sudden vigour. 'There's only one sure thing—those last ones that lived here had no money, otherwise they wouldn't've let the place go to pot the way they done—did. I was warned I'd find it in pretty bad shape, when I took it over.' Abruptly and decisively, as I'd done earlier, she changed the subject. 'What've you done with the rest of the flat? I'd be int'rested to see.'

I'd been waiting for that, of course, but my heart didn't sink any the less. But no help for it; on the heels of her question, that sounded like a virtual challenge, she'd levered herself up out of her chair and stood waiting. Accordingly, the two of us set forth. Yet all during our tour of inspection that other thing dogged me, the same as when we'd talked about the house—my impression that she knew rather more than she was telling, and that this reticence was not only deliberate but calculated; designed to screen some purpose of her own that she held in reserve, though for the life of me I couldn't think what.

So to her greedy curiosity, companioned by her ominous and deepening silence, I displayed the two simple but pleasant bedrooms, mine with the sewing-machine in it, and the shining little kitchen, all gay and new. It was the sight of the bathroom however that brought her envy, resentment, hostility—whichever it was, maybe a mixture of all three—to a head. I don't apologize either for being a bit sybaritic in that department, Christabel and I share the same dread of a cold bathroom; there's nothing more unhealthy. In the same thickening silence she surveyed the warm cork floor, the pale blue fitments, the thick woolen rugs, basin and pedestal, all brightly lit and warm as toast, with its own miniature Dimplex.

'Well!' the sight brought from her in a voice corrosive as verdigris. 'You certainly believe in making yourselves comfortable, don't you?'

'Well, I'm not young.' Propitiatingly I evaded the insolence. 'I find I do need warmth for my poor old bones, I get such bad colds if I'm chilled.' (A lie.)

This silenced without appeasing her, and again I'd the sense—more strongly than before—that she was incubating something. And sure enough, the moment we'd got back to the living-room, out it came.

'Did you know,' she smirked, 'there was a murder in this house?'

Well! it struck me dumb. Literally, actually dumb, I don't mind telling you. The *malice* of it! for that's all it was, pure malice. She knew perfectly well that many people, knowing such a thing of a house, would be put off it completely, and how did she know that Christabel and I wouldn't feel that way too? She was getting even with me for the attractiveness of our flat, that was all; springing it on me like that out of contemptible spite—an attack which I encountered with a nonchalance that would keep her (I hoped) from seeing how unpleasantly disturbed I was.

'Dear me!' My voice was light and composed, even faintly amused. 'Not recently, I hope?'

'Well—no.' By the disappearance of her evil smile you could see her disappointment—that her benevolent little plan hadn't come off. 'Not what you'd call recently.'

'When?' I felt I must pin this intelligence just a bit. 'When was this?'

'Well, a hundred years ago, anyway.' Like most people of her class she had slovenly concepts of time, and no precise grip of facts. 'Maybe over a hundred.'

'And who was murdered? Man? woman? child?'

'A woman, it's supposed to be.' Her land-mine having fizzled out damply, she'd lost interest.

'The house isn't haunted.' It'd come out of me plump, like that, without premeditation. Also I'd made the mistake of stating it as a fact, not asking about it, and of course my positive tone made her come straight back at me with, 'I should say *not*. What put haunting into your head?'

Well, naturally I wasn't going to tell *her* of my gift,

51

nor that even in its suppressed and disused state it would've told me straightaway of any haunting. So I said blandly, 'Oh, it's just that I don't believe you'd have bought the house and made your part of it so charming, if there were any talk of its being haunted. That sort of rumour, if it gets about, keeps a house empty more or less forever, wouldn't you say?'

She grunted, neither yes nor no. I understood her frame of mind exactly; she only wanted to get away and churn her bile in solitude over our iniquitous luxury, and over her failure to alarm me with her tale of murder. But I wasn't having any of that, thank you, I wasn't letting her off so easily. She deserved a bit of punishment for trying to spoil our home for us—when we'd only just moved in, too—and what's more my last remark had inspired me; I knew exactly how I was going to twist the knife.

'It's so *fascinating!*' I cried with rapture. 'A murder mystery! *Do* sit down, my dear Mrs. Rumbold, and tell me *all* about it!'

'I don't know any more'n I've told you.' She was sullen, disgruntled, her eyes moving restlessly toward the door. 'I'll have to be going now, I—'

'Oh not yet, *please* not yet,' I insisted between gush and clamour. 'Just one more cup of tea, I'm sure you'll remember more about it while we're chatting. Do sit down just a few moments more, please.'

After a pause—and how unwillingly I can't tell you— she sat. She was too gauche, too utterly without social grace, to extricate herself neatly and pleasantly. And I sat down too and filled her cup and never stopped talking for one moment, and I spared her nothing—I promise you.

'Was it the husband?' I twittered, 'who killed his wife?'

'What I know about it's damn all,' she said gruffly. 'I've told you.'

'Oh, Mrs. Rumbold!' I fluted all at once, in my highest ingenue register. 'I've just had the most *marvelous* idea! In places like Clapham, that used to be small country villages, there's always a pretty long local memory of crime or violence. Suppose I ask about it in the neighbourhood—'

'*What!*'

'—and find out whether the house has any reputation of being haunted—'

'I'll thank you,' she broke in shrilly, 'to do nothing of the kind!'

'I only mean,' I prattled artlessly, 'find out if there's any tradition of a murder followed by a haunting, that's all, just as a matter of int—'

'No!'

She was all but shouting—glaring too, undisguisedly. The thought of such enquiries being set in motion, and the harm they might do to the value of her property, had brought her bursting from her sullenness like froth from a bottle of beer.

'Put questions about like that,' she was saying fiercely, 'and first thing you know they'll be saying the house *is* haunted—and no end of fools t'keep saying it! Miss Teasdale, if you—'

She controlled herself just short (you could tell) of menace, and compelled herself unwillingly to less violent forms of speech.

'—I'm asking you as a favour,' she pursued less heatedly but still forcibly, 'never to go mentioning any such thing anywhere, least of all hereabouts where we've got to live. Not *ever!*'

53

'But of *course* I shouldn't, if you object,' I cooed, dovelike. 'I shouldn't *dream* of going against your wishes. Do have another sandwich.'

'No more, thanks.—Give a place that sort of name,' she reverted to her grievance, 'and who'd take anything in it, rent-free? Not that giving free rents is any plan of me and my daughter, I'm telling you!'

'But don't worry, don't worry, I shan't say a word, I promise you, I swear.—Oh!' I was all beaming and happy with another bright idea. 'Suppose you and I go to a quite remarkable medium I know, we could ask if there'd actually been a murder here, or even get in touch with the murdered woman—'

'No!' she bayed with all her lungs, in full and sweeping refusal. 'I've never had any dealings with truck like that and I never will, I don't believe in it—!'

'Well then I shan't, of course I shan't. One of these nice little cakes, Mrs. Rumbold? Just one, please do—'

'No, no more. Just don't start anything with mediums, don't go talking haunts, none of that stuff—'

It took a number of promises amounting to oaths of silence before she got from her chair and plunged massively out of the door—still pursued by furies, you could tell; still plowed with worry that my indiscreet talk might spoil her renting prospects. Yes, but she'd been willing to spoil our flat for *us*, with that story of hers. Sauce for the goose—but expect a woman of her type to see it that way. My suggestion of a medium, I may add, had been pure fabrication; breaking off contact with anyone like that had been part of my plan of severance, years ago.

Once she'd gone I could have my little laugh out, thinking how she'd squirmed on the hook and how I'd kept her squirming. And I don't apologize for gloating a bit, either; if anyone'd ever asked for it, she had.

Then I saw I'd a problem—to tell my niece about the episode, or not. And after thinking for some moments, I decided not. You can't predict individual reactions to things, however well you think you know a person; it might just be that this legendary murder would affect her with some flickering unease, some nagging pinpoint of distaste she couldn't get rid of. So the more I thought, the more firmly I decided not to bother her with any part of it, my dear dearest girl. Slaving over the flat evenings as she'd done for weeks, already tired out from her daytime job. . . .

That disposed of, I found myself—incorrigibly—mulling over the so-called murder, for all its vagueness. First of all I didn't for one moment believe that the Rumbold woman had invented it; she hadn't that much imagination, or what she did have would be like her malice—dull and coarse, incapable of invention. Obviously she was repeating something she'd heard, some rumour at some foggy remove, and probably kicking herself for having done it, too. All in all it amounted to nothing most likely, not worth another moment's thought. . . .

And yet—for all my immaculate reasoning—my mere absorption in the period kept me touching, here and there, on various points and patterns. *A hundred years ago*, she'd said, *more than a hundred*. It sounded eighteen-sixtyish, the Victorian age in its fullest bloom of glossy surfaces, consenting hypocrisies, and the abysses beneath. Well: of Mrs. Rumbold's narrative, one thing I could say for sure. This murder, assuming there'd been one, must have been in too drab a social stratum or too devoid of gruesomeness in itself, to attract even contemporary attention;

otherwise it would have been written up extensively, with murderer and murdered taking their rightful places at Mme. Tussaud's. The classic Victorian cases—Adelaide Bartlett, Constance Kent, the Balham mystery, the Penge atrocity—all these have been worked over again and again, even by such marvellous writers as the historian-novelist Elizabeth Jenkins. And among these time-honoured exhibits, petrified in words and in wax, no Clapham murder had any place, at least that I'd ever heard of.

For, let me tell you, I'm an *insatiable* reader in that period, all the way from Cyril Pearl's diamond-paved courtesans at £5,000 a night, down to Mayhew and Dickens carrying their lanterns into the stenches of direst and blackest poverty. If I revel in the Marchioness of Londonderry, coal-heiress and the richest woman in England, I don't forget Mayhew's poor drab collecting dogs' excrement for the tanners of leather; I'm fascinated by the splendours and the horrors, both. So as I say, if I've never come across any outstanding murder named for this area, I could be moderately sure there'd never been one. Some domestic quarrel at most, with an ugly but unpremeditated ending? Some violence among social nobodies, totally unproductive of delicious scandal?

Finally it occurred to me (I'd got to the yawning stage rather) that whatever had happened, hadn't even happened in this house. What with the dimming and blurring of time, it might have taken place in some other long-vanished 'villa' in this once semi-rural neighbourhood.

Or if it turned out to be the case, I shouldn't be in the least surprised.

Have you a few special moments that you treasure in your mind? Moments of happiness and sweetness impervious to time and change, shining with their own inner light? Well, the evening after the Rumbold visitation—perhaps by contrast—stands in my memory like that, golden and perfect forever. It was fairly late and we were reading on either side of the fireplace, electric alas but glowing; the room warm as toast, the light from our two parchment-shaded lamps bright yet mild. That's how it stands in my mind, as inviolable in its peace, order and content as one of those paintings of old Dutch interiors.

I'd an idea it was raining, actually, but was far too comfortable and lazy to go and see. Now and again I'd raise my head and let my eyes range about the walls, for which Christabel had achieved a subdued buff with a soft, dim, golden quality. Already the room looked mellow as if lived in a long time and as if—smile if you like—it knew it'd woken from long degradation to find itself cherished and loved. And the balm of it, the repose, sank through my tired bones into my very soul. Our flat in Chelsea had been so nice and so terribly convenient for us both; the raw shock and distress of being turfed out of it—with no real certainty that we'd find anything both acceptable and within our means—were receding from me, but could still be brought alive at a touch. Homelessness for anyone, but for older women most of all, I expect, is a nightmare—Oh it's too terrible, I try now not to think of it and tried not to then, to think instead of this lovely room and be grateful. . . .

At that moment the clock struck ten with its sweet tingling voice; I believe it's a very good one actually, from a great-grandmother on our side of the family. While it was still chiming Christabel raised her head from her reading, and her eyes met mine.

'We *are* getting the room banged into shape, aren't

we?' she said with that affinity of thought that seems to exist between us so often. 'And we'll still do things to it, lots.'

I gave a nod and smile, half-drowsy.

'Nice, isn't it?' She was smiling too. 'Nice to have a *home*?'

Having echoed my own thought once more she returned to the auction catalogue in which she was ticking off items. I watched her down-bent head and her absorption for another moment until—all at once—I remembered something she'd forgotten to do. So I did it, quickly and furtively.

Touched wood.

I woke next morning at ten o'clock. Ten o'clock, on a weekday! It'd been years, literally, since I'd indulged in such luxuriousness—holidays excepted, of course. We'd gone to bed quite early, about eleven, and I must have slept like a log straight through—the effect, I suppose, of my soporific contented evening, my lulling sense of happiness and new security.

And yet—lying there thinking about opening my eyes, preparing myself for the relentless effort of sitting up, pushing the bed-clothes back, evicting my legs from the warmth and shelter—I was detained all at once by a feeling of trouble, small and remote but stubborn. It was strong enough to immobilize me for another few moments, trying to isolate it. Why in heaven's name too, why on this morning of all mornings when I should be upspringing like the lark—as far as practicable, I mean, for a slightly-arthritic spinster in her sixties? It was odd, though, how urgently I wanted to define it . . . no go, however, couldn't put my finger on it. I concluded at last that it must be the vague oppression that follows an unpleasant but unremembered dream, or perhaps only a slight headache from oversleeping, and evicted myself briskly from under the blankets.

The flat was silent, my girl'd gone to work long since. In dressing-gown and slippers I made breakfast and carried the tray to the refectory table in the corner of the living-room that was also our dining area, and sat over coffee and toast and marmalade at leisure, savouring the tranquillity and the peace. No treadmill of obligation, no batterings to endure from the captiousness or caprice of female customers. . . .

In the same blissful vacuous leisure I dressed and strolled out, to find a breath of spring in the March air—you know how it comes all at once like an unexpected present, the air suddenly mild, the sun suddenly warm, the faces suddenly smiling with the pleasure of it—and did a little shopping in the High Street, enjoying the throngs that moved in the current of morning, still lively and fresh. When I'd got back I tidied what remained to tidy, pottered a little here, a little there—till I came up hard against the thing hidden till then: the barrier with nothing beyond it, nothing *next*. . . .

It was only now that the true nature of my waking unease caught up with me, in all its baneful simplicity. You *can't* read all morning and all afternoon, you can't potter for six or eight hours on end, you sit wearing yourself out at the hardest work there is—wondering how to kill time. And I'm not *used* to killing time, I'm not used to being without occupation or purpose, and I knew at once I couldn't endure it. Ungrateful, you're saying? and this soon? You're quite right. All the same, here was the very first day of my holiday, and my way of enjoying it was to sit there with my nerves all of a twitch. I was under orders from Christabel of course, strict orders to rest, and with the best will in the world to disobey her, I didn't know how to set about it. So I sat and looked my bankruptcy in the face. Nothing to do; nothing to do all day.

So there I was, looking disconsolately into the street with its shut-up depositories, a scene whose barrenness of life, movement, interest, echoed my own barrenness. And how much more of this vacuum before Dancey would need me? Three months of it Christabel had said, *three months?* As good as a prison sentence (and you'll see later how ironic that was) but already I was panicking, literally panicking . . . and at that moment an odd little thing happened: Mrs. Rumbold irrupted into the forefront of my mind like a flung stone, in preternaturally sharp and vivid detail as if hit by a spotlight. And nothing to account for it either, nothing had been farther from my thoughts, but all the same there she stood in the fierce distinctness, that *immediacy* . . . and as if her apparition had been some sort of herald or prophecy, below me came the sound of the front door closing and the woman herself going down the walk, carrying a shopping-bag.

At once I was on my feet, by mere reflex. The sight of her, and implications of the sight, raced through my mind like a series of exploding flashes, one after the other. Yet again I can swear to you I'd not been dreaming of such a thing even remotely, I *swear* it. But with irresistible force, as the pictured woman materialized in the act of absenting herself, other pictures raced past me with dizzying, intoxicating speed. Her months-old allusion to neglected and untouched attics; the evident purpose of her departure, virtual guarantee against any sudden reappearance; the empty for the better part of an hour, empty, *empty*. . . .

My breath came short, my body shook with the violent pounding of my heart and the violence of my speculation, equally. Here was my chance to pursue the problematical murder, to prove or even *dis*prove it. But such a family disaster, if the family had lived in this house—surely it must have rent their lives sufficiently to leave *some* token in its wake, allusions, scars? or even significant gaps? the lesions of omission, the suggestiveness of silence . . . ?

And all the same, strung tight for action as I was, I faltered. Privacy's still a powerful instinct with people of my generation; ferreting of any sort, prying stealthily into the affairs of others, is foreign to my nature, or at least I like to think it is. The whole idea had been a chimera, a candle lit by my despair of idleness and going out now, guttering into a thread of smoke. How could I have imagined I could carry it through, anyway? Give it up for the hallucination it was, let it go once and for all. And what peace it was to have decided, what a relief. Until—

Until I saw the note, originally propped against the clock on the mantel and fallen down flat; something I could have missed indefinitely if it hadn't happened, just in that moment, to catch my eye.

> Lorna—Alec's taking us out to dinner to cel-
> ebrate the new flat, he asked me yesterday and
> I forgot to tell you, sorry. We'll pick you up at
> seven, I shan't have time to change but you be
> bootiful for both of us.

So there, bang, went my one little hope of activity—pre-paring dinner—in all the lifeless puddle of the day; you don't know how I'd been treasuring the prospect. And at once—with all restraints against it withdrawn—my hungry curiosity came flooding back, hungrier than ever; a dizzy excitement tuned up and up so unbearably high I felt that something must topple over, or snap. . . . I was out into the hall and up the stairs without knowing how I'd got there, hardly. I was blank, empty, an automaton moving outside itself and possessed by one single thought, one single purpose. . . .

In the second floor hall, changelessly silent and untouched, I paused to get my bearings. The plan of this particular type of old house, whether on a large or small scale, is substantially the same; there'd have to be a door obviously unrelated to the file of bedroom doors on the right. I found it toward the rear of the hall as I'd expected, on the left-hand side. I hurried toward it on guilty ridiculous tiptoe, and to my relief found it unlocked; not that I'd specially anticipated formidable locks protecting what could only be accumulations of junk. I turned the shaky knob and pulled it open on the expected vista of narrow wooden steps going up steeply, with a dangerously sharp twist as they approached the top landing. Having negotiated the twist, I stood for another moment and reconnoitred. To my right a mean little passage ran toward the front of the house. Along it were four closed doors, shabby and low; up here the ceiling was very low. Quickly and cautiously I opened all four and peered in. Four dim cubicles with tiny windows, completely opaque with dust; four pallet beds with ragged collapsed ticking on them fuzzed with vague all-over desiccation, probably the souvenir of straw stuffing; four rickety chests of drawers, four flimsy chairs, four gas-jets; some cobwebby traces at the windows, once possibly curtains—all left just as it was, perhaps, when the last cook and housemaids had packed their small tin trunks and gone, who knows how long ago. At least the 1930 inheritors hadn't had resident servants, at least not by the look of these quarters.

This exploration being accomplished merely for the sake of thoroughness, I retraced my steps to the landing and the solitary door that gave access, obviously, to the rear half of the floor. Its knob was hanging loose, the flimsy portal itself gave a dry old creak and groan combined as I pushed it half open, put my head around it cautiously and —for all my prognosis of mould and decay—stood completely daunted, at least for the moment.

My first over-all impression was of a dirty turbulence, arrested in mid-motion; ankle-deep at least; moveless eruptions not only of rubbish but of *mean* rubbish; even the larger pieces one could see, in their prime, as having emerged from the lowest depths of Victorian taste. And buried in these evidences of some well-to-do tradesman's mental and spiritual level, Mrs. Rumbold expected to find Italian primitives or First Folios or Charles II silver? *Enough to make your heart sink*, she'd said of the attic; to that extent at least she'd been right.

I went on staring, nothing else to do after that first full stop of futility; staring and staring, trying to impose some form upon formlessness, trying to extort any impression at all from chaos and debris. I had to; if I didn't, nothing for it but to return to the flat, the lonely, empty, occupationless flat. . . .

The thought of it restiffened my purpose and renewed my effort of observation; by now my eyes had made vague distinctions in this tumbled geography of litter. Dismiss the broken chairs, dismiss the rickety wash-stands and an unmistakable commode, dismiss the broken-backed sofa in hideous embossed plush gone mouldy; the one outstanding object in the room was a big old wardrobe seeming to lean forward a little from the right-hand wall. No mystery about it either, with its left-hand door sagging wide open, tilting away drunkenly from its broken upper hinge. Nothing whatever hung from some rusty hooks inside it, but irregular humps of something lay at the bottom. I picked my way toward it and saw under a furry blanket of dust the vague outlines of . . . books by the look of it, dumped without even an attempt at stacking? I was just about to penetrate the blanket a little, at random, when belated caution brought me upright again, for necessary reflection.

True, I'd seen our landlady leave the house; I'd no immediate need to scramble or listen for approaching footsteps with my heart in my mouth. On the other hand I put her down as a type unlikely to prolong her absence with such little frivolities as a cup of coffee somewhere; with her watchdog temperament she'd always want to get home as soon as possible. I'd ample time, but not unlimited time for this first exploration and for others; I must remember that. So at once, resolutely, I bent to the vague mounds and tumbled them a bit. At once their smell rose from under their disturbed shroud and bit acridly in my nostrils, that peculiar necrotic smell of decayed paper. Books, as their outlines had foretold; nondescript dumpy volumes, cheap editions of novels or sermons. Beneath the top lot, though, a far more massive outline revealed itself, a tome of formidable bulk. I pulled it free, hardly creating movement or displacement among the others, which seemed actually adhering one to the other.

Having secured the ponderous object I stood clasping it, regardless of its filthy condition; thinking, with new urgency, that it was high time I went. *She* wasn't back yet, her habit of banging doors should reach me even up here, but it was foolish to leave my escape till the very last moment; I could see myself falling head over heels down those corkscrew stairs in my hurry, with the twin possibilities of discovery and broken bones . . . no, not to be thought of. Also I'm not too sure on my feet any more, my speed's less than it used to be and also—more lethally—I can't trust my balance. Old age of course, but provoking.

So with deliberation, very carefully and quietly, I picked my way back to the door. Just as I was closing it behind me I happened to glance along the passage, and had the disagreeable shock of seeing my footprints clearly outlined in the dust. I could even see other vague tracks—she herself had been up here, she'd said—but of course those earlier traces were partly dust-filled and faint. How to meet this unforeseen emergency I didn't know, so for the moment I had to take a chance and do nothing. She didn't come here much, by her own account; my prints would have time to merge with hers, or at least I could hope. . . .

So clutching the volume and setting my feet down with extremest caution I crept downstairs; the silence of the house was unbroken as I let myself into the flat. Only then did I realize how my heart was pounding, and stood still to let it subside; all the while, unconsciously, still hugging my loot to my bosom. My hands were filthy black, my fairly nice dress was begrimed past brushing. That dust-blanket in the attic was different from any dust I'd ever seen, a sort of felt that looked damp and *was* damp, actually, to the touch; I can't understand why, but it was. And meanwhile I'd begun bustling about, spreading fresh paper towels on a table and dumping the book upon it; then I got to work with more paper towels very slightly dampened, and what came off on the first half-dozen of them was mud more than anything else, coal black mud. Up to the last of these purifications, to tell you the truth, its thickness and weight had suggested to me only one thing; I kept expecting to see Holy Bible come swimming up through the dust-veil in those hideous Gothic letters that so invoke the dismal machine-made Gothic of the period. And I'd *welcome* a Bible, I'd consider it treasure-trove; from its register of births, marriages and deaths, meticulously kept according to the fashion of the day, I'd glean *names*, a starting-point from which I might build up, little by little, this forgotten family and its involvement or otherwise in equally-forgotten murder. Suppose that even the name of the victim might emerge, or clues to the other one, the *other*. . . .

Trembling inwardly, my hands shaking with the effort of restrained haste, I wiped and wiped carefully at the strong intact covers a good half-inch thick, deeply arabesqued with florid designs in contrasting grained and glossy surfaces. Brass clasps, tarnished black, held it shut. Naturally I'd begun to realize that the tome couldn't be what I'd thought, and the first clear sight of its compressed edges—gilt-edged once and a good bit of it left—offered additional evidence. No Bible, however ponderous, ever had cardboard pages. And when I'd pried open the reluctant clasps there it was, in mint condition—something that no one had so much as glanced at, I was sure, for the last seventy or eighty years at least.

Fascinated, gloating, I stared at it lying open before me. In its expanse of heavily-padded mounting, still brilliantly white and barely yellowed at the edges, were set four ovals surrounded with an embossed flower-and-vine pattern in high relief. All four contained faded portraits of women in half or three-quarter length, posed beside ornamental fern stands or similar, against canvas backgrounds of balustraded terraces. All of them seemed to be in what the Victorians regarded as advanced middle life—thirty-five to forty-five—and all seemed rather dreary types with no vestige of anything interesting or individual. Beneath each oval was a date, a Christian name, and absolutely nothing else. The same was true of other pages I glanced at, and presumably would be true throughout the album—sundry Catherines and Adelaides with an occasional stodgy James or John and, later on, a series of a child in various stages of growth. In a family circle no last names would be needed, but all the same I couldn't suppress a rising sense of injury. A Bible, now, would have given Christian, family and married names; on the other hand, it wouldn't offer likenesses. What I had before me was at the same time more informative, and less informative, than a written record. Still, one mustn't cry for the moon. . . .

Already rebuffed as it were, yet riveted, I continued opening pages very carefully and gently. No need actually, the album wasn't in the least fragile but good as new; regarded in its day, no doubt, as an object of artistic value to be cherished. Some of the boards were lightly stuck together—nothing that a letter-opener couldn't coax apart.

By the time I'd got part way through the gallery, though, I'd acquired nothing but more discontents. It'd begun to strike me that most of the earlier pictures might have been what I believe was called a *calotype*. Whether this process was more apt to fade than others, I couldn't say; all I do know is that the faces were too dim for recognition, and the women's identities were literally extinguished by their elaborate ruffled caps, with big muslin bows foaming under the chin. Persistent anonymity, so discouraging and disappointing. . . .

For lack of anything better I began following up the

single variation in the monotony, the child. Her first appearance was at the age of two or thereabout, clutching a tin pail and shovel against canvas sand and salt sea waves. *Annabel, 1850.* Later, a demure Alice-like doll, she sat pretty as could be on a lacy white iron bench; the canvas background was now a marble balustrade, additionally garnished with marble urns and a peacock. *Annabel, 1856.* Both as baby and little girl her beauty was evident—that wonderful childish beauty that's so apt to disappear at seven or eight. Yet in what I'd guess as her tenth year and later, it was still in brightest petally flowering—and the current little-girl style, glossy curls, bare shoulders, airy muslin skirts and a tiny satin apron, didn't do her looks any harm that you could notice.

Still, for what it was worth, it was a clue of sorts. The family had had children or at least *a* child born about 1848 or '49. Her successive appearances as she grew up were under a shortened name; all labeled in the same small slanting hand as in her babyhood, all done with that same care at once meticulous and uniformative. *Belle, 1863; Belle, 1865.* How did that sort of thing help me? What I needed was some means of *attaching* this girl somewhere; of seeing her with her parents and brothers and sisters, if any had come later; of seeing her properly placed in the family frame. A group was my imperious necessity now, anything that would help me sort these people into their various relationships. I turned pages more and more rapidly, ignoring individual portraits for the time being. A group, there had to be at least one; any family of the period would have had themselves taken as a group. . . .

Aha!
At last, and in the very heart of the album—the central

mounts regally reserved for the family in stately assemblages—on one single large mount, precisely the sort of thing I was looking for. My first act, as it were surreptitiously, was to snatch glances farther on and make sure that this big photograph wasn't the only one, so that I could wallow luxuriously in the thought of pleasures to come. Other groups did follow, but even on such hasty scrutiny it seemed to me—and I was right as it happened —that the variations of pose weren't important enough to matter.

So my first procedure, with the original group, was to scan it as a whole, saving up my finer dissection of personalities as a *bonne bouche*. And oh bliss, all the faces here weren't retreating from me into the dim past where I couldn't follow, but were clear black and white; distinct, unmistakable and individual. Of course by its date, 1865, photographic techniques were already incomparably better; really superb likenesses were being achieved by the fifties and sixties.

And yes, here was one such achievement, an example that might serve as the classic pattern of the middling tradesman's family, offering their display of heavy middling prosperity to the lens as they sat in their garden. House in the background, unmistakably this same house except that it possessed rather handsome shutters at that time, which gave it a much more ornate look; four female servants in blurred background focus, grouped standing on the front steps; on the left a rough middle-aged type and a rough juvenile type, obviously the gardener and gardener's boy.

Now all this, to a lover of the period, was eloquent of the family's means and standard of living. Four women servants, regulation in any middle-class family, but no man-servant; a gardener but no coachman, which meant no carriage. This they would hire on occasion from what was known as a jobbing liveryman. Actually the photograph was a set-piece—perfect and precise, like wax-work —of a retired tradesman's establishment. No culture, no style, no elegance, only a gross plenty; the women filling dead days by over-eating and over-dressing and embroidering fire-screens or playing badly on the piano, harp or mandolin. And now, having confirmed a general impression, I could settle down to particular inspections; take each separate face and try to extort the secret of its character, dwell upon it, go into trances and *brood*. . . .

The five unknowns confronting me with such assured (as it were) distinctness, were separated from the blurred servants on the doorstep by a driveway; from its sweeping curve you could tell there'd been a large front garden, before the mean suburban street came and sheared it off. And there in the line-up, sure enough, was the solitary wretched male drowned in females. Four of them! I bent closer, intent on assigning them their roles. On his right sat a massive woman, darkly pompous and on her dignity, and I surprised myself by saying aloud, 'Good day to you, Mrs. Rumbold!' It *was* amusing, the resemblance—not a physical one actually, but a striking resemblance of *type*. This pictured one I took for being exactly what she looked —over-bearing, purse-proud and coarse with it; fond of throwing her weight about. *The wife*, I thought, with a twinge of sympathy for the husband; if it turned out that he'd murdered her, I felt that he had good grounds. Then I progressed to the woman at his left, an overweight listless creature in the late thirties or early forties, whose drooping frame seemed unequal to the weight of her rich voluminous dress, absolutely *clotted* with tasteless trimmings. Beside her, again, sat another female whom I skipped over lightly as being the usual poor relation, diffident and no longer young and obviously—of these five presences—the least important. And in front of these four mature bodies was the girl, sitting on the grass or on an invisible footstool. Fourteen or fifteen she'd be by now, still the only child of the family it appeared, and prettier than ever; not wearing a cap of course, not at her age. The petrified solemnity of her elders was probably a consequence of the stillness then necessary for the long exposures. Last of all, I returned to the man; for all the husband's absolute authority in that day, I somehow felt that he hardly counted. Physically he'd a strong square frame and square features with thick mutton-chops; a bit pompous, a bit slow, but not ill-natured. Solid as Gibraltar he sat in his fine black suit and heavy silk cravat, with the thick links of a watch-chain draped across his well-nourished front. Rather common maybe and capable of being extremely stubborn; not of anything worse than that, or so I judged.

And so, and so; having achieved a first reconnaissance of the party, I found I'd also achieved a series of labels, just trial identifications. Reading from left to right, the wife, the husband; one sister of husband or wife, widowed most likely and rich; one sister of husband or wife, spinsterish-looking and obviously poor, the family's dogsbody; one young daughter of the house, as spoiled as she was pretty by the look of her.

Having got this far I moved back again to the head of the line, the wife, only then realizing how definitely I'd marked her for the victim; that her insufferable domineering haughtiness had goaded her husband to some fatal violence seemed entirely reasonable. While smiling in token reproof at my leap in the dark and staring at her all the while, I saw what I hadn't seen before. Clearly visible at either side of her neck, flowing down behind her from her portentous cap, were the unconfined bands then called weepers. A widow's cap; a widow. I should have noticed before, likewise, the encrustations all over her dress, thick deposits of jet wherever jet could be applied. And with that discovery, I saw something else—the strong family resemblance between this armoured tank of a widow, and the man. He didn't have her offensive and consequential look, but the structure of the faces was similar and their bodies were alike—except that his fat had gone into his belly and hers into her enormous bosom. So: the husband's rich widowed sister, and by her assured and authoritative look she was a permanent member of the household—an acquisition, I should think, of doubtful value. It was the flaccid over-dressed creature on his *left* who was the wife, as her central position in the group should have told me anyhow.

And now, as if all these revised impressions of mine had somehow shaken the whole group into a new alignment—into new focus as it were—I began to see other things I'd been blind to before. Now that I'd begun to unlock these graven images from their photographic catalepsy, I could see the resemblance between the wife and the faded woman next to her, the one I'd called dogsbody. They even seemed to lean toward each other very slightly, as if for mutual reassurance and protection; sisters I'd say, beyond doubt. The wife's face was utterly apathetic, but the other's. . . .

Yes, the other's; now that I accorded her the courtesy of a real look it seemed to me I could trace, behind that timid and self-effacing look, something spirited at one time, perhaps even spiritual or at least highly intelligent.

It was possible likewise that in her youth she'd been extremely attractive, even rather outstanding. She wasn't tight and glossy with over-feeding like the rest, but too thin actually, hollow-chested. Through her evident awareness of her humble status something shone out that the others didn't possess, a native delicacy and fineness. The poor relation in her unfashionably scanty dress with its scanty ruffles, the eater of the bread of charity . . . And yet, as my glance traversed the group over and over and came back to her, she seemed to me—more and more—to be the only person worth looking at.

So, once more: the husband's *rich* widowed sister, the wife's *poor* widowed sister. How glad I was that the poor one'd been lucky enough to find a home with a prosperous relation, although—on further scrutiny—the prosperous relation didn't look all that flourishing herself. Listless, almost vacant-looking, far too plump but limp and flabby, she seemed as much in need of a sheltering arm as her pathetic sister; chronically ailing, I'd guess, from hermetically sealed bedrooms and gluts of rich food. *She* was the lucky one perhaps in that her husband allowed her family dependent to live in his house. And I mean 'allowed' literally; please remember that every penny a wife possessed, every dress and every trinket, belonged to her husband to squander or sell or give to another woman if he chose. The husband in this particular case seemed good-natured enough as it happened, but if he'd turned ugly about supporting an encumbrance, what could his wife do about it? If a woman fell into bad hands through marriage God help her, for the laws of her country certainly wouldn't. . . .

I broke off, amazed at my silliness. Here I was, working

73

myself into a lather over the imagined plight of unknown people, on first glimpse at that; better cool off. . . .

I went on turning pages. There were four other groups, obviously taken on the same occasion, though the backgrounds had shifted. First to a conservatory that must once have looked into a large rear garden, cloudily visible through the glass; then to a parlour, posed against a mantel smothered in swags of drapery and displaying an ornate clock hideous beyond belief. In the parlour pose, the wife had her hand affectionately tucked into her sister's arm; you could just see two fingers of it among the ruffles. More to the point, there was now a clear view of the Poor Sister's left hand. Ringless; a spinster therefore, not a widow; the classic Victorian dependent, literally homeless and penniless otherwise.

As for the girl, she stood out with charming, almost brilliant emphasis against the background of sombre adults. She'd refined features and a splendid lot of shining ringlets tumbling about her shoulders, with virginal intimations of the exquisite figure to come. What made her *really* appealing though—irresistibly appealing—was her gay and confident smile, that certitude of hope so untarnished and so touchingly *young*. Her looks clearly came from her mother's side of the family, in fact they suggested to me what the mother and especially the Poor Sister must have been in their youth. And I was glad likewise that this girl took after her mother and the poor aunt, not the arrogant rich one. . . .

But this wasn't what slowed my hands between one page and the next, while imposing an even greater slowness—a full stop—on my imagination. Assuming that Mrs. Rumbold's tale of murder in this house wasn't mere local exaggeration but had some basis in actual fact, you can see my problem. Where—in this line-up of persons so intensely conventional and respectable—*where* find a murderer? The torpid husband? the drooping apathetic wife? the purse-proud widow of the black looks? the spinster who offered her faint propitiating smile like a withered olive-branch? the light-hearted young girl? All impossible on the face of it, or at least so improbable as to be ridiculous. Or given a murderer, who was the victim? Equally difficult role to assign; equally absurd. As I gaped at them, pitting conjecture against a stone wall, I happened to glance at my wrist.

You'd think I'd been shot, the way I jumped up. It couldn't be late as this, so late in the afternoon . . . it was though and no mistake, I'd none too much time to bathe and dress and polish up the living-room a bit and arrange a tray with sherry and glasses. Incredible how the hours—the dreaded empty hours—had slipped away while I sat entranced, letting myself be drawn into the orbit of lives long vanished . . . and Oh dear I'd intended to go out and buy a few flowers, they give such a lift to a room; with all day to do it in, I hadn't even done that.

I bundled the album into my wardrobe and thrust it toward the very end of the floor. Later, as I took a last hasty survey of myself in the mirror (little enough to detain me there, I promise you) I realized something so joyful as to be actually startling. My dreaded month of leisure with its dreaded idleness, loneliness . . . but now no more dread, none, none. Now that I'd opened this new little vein of interest, of even improbable mystery, my whole mood was transformed like magic. The extent of the blessing hadn't quite sunk in yet, there'd been no time, but now it came home to me in all its fullness. Now I was seeing in my mind's eye the empty silent flat, all mine after Christabel's departure, and myself absorbed, riveted, buried deep in my quest for Victorian gore. And I had to smile, when I thought how I'd dreaded solitude. Dread it? *now*? I was panting for it, I was hungry for solitude; I couldn't wait.

Mr. Sterrett took us to a nice small restaurant in the King's Road, very homely outside and very expensive inside; excellent Italian-French cooking served on bare wooden tables, scrubbed white. I like him, I've always liked him. He has a good strong figure, medium-tall, and a good head of black hair with a lot of grey in it, very becoming to his rather angular dark face. A serious face naturally, but you should see how it lights up when he smiles, and makes him almost young. He dresses well in a conservative way; not that he's conservative by nature, apart from his rather intimidating common sense. He's painfully in love with Christabel; I've seen it get away from him sometimes, when he looks at her. Not very often though, he's a self-controlled, sober and mature man. Oh how, how I wish she'd return his feeling; if only she were married to him, secure and cherished forever . . . no chance of it though, no chance whatever.

'He's in love with you,' I'd ventured to say once, long ago. I knew I was taking a liberty, but I couldn't help myself. From the very first he'd struck me as kind and intelligent, well bred and well read, the sort of man one doesn't meet too often; a man who'd be not only a devoted husband but an interesting companion. So as I say, I'd taken a chance of being thoroughly snubbed in remarking, 'He's in love with you.'

'As if I didn't know.' She was perfectly off-hand, just

going on with something she was drawing; I could have smacked her.

'Well, I think he's charming.' She was silent and I ventured further, not having been rebuffed at once. 'I can't imagine anyone nicer.'

'Oh yes, he's nice,' she returned absently. 'Old Sobersides.'

'Yes,' I returned waspishly. 'He doesn't strum an electric guitar nor sing American Negro songs in cockney.'

'A widower,' she disposed of him casually. 'Who wants it?'

'Even so.' I had to restrain my annoyance with her, of which I was feeling plenty. 'Would you prefer one room with a hairy youth who smells, and last week's dishes in the sink?'

'Oh Lord.' She began to laugh. 'I've been asked to share I don't know how many scruffy establishments, and you notice I've managed to decline, so far—?'

'But don't you want to marry at all?' It burst out of me, I couldn't help it. 'Not ever?'

She actually raised her head from the drawing-board, and thought a moment.

'I've thought of marriage now and again. But never—' her reflectiveness changed to conviction '—never of what I expect from marriage. I've never thought of that.'

'And may one ask your ladyship—' I'd gone vinegary, and I couldn't help that either '—when you intend to begin thinking?'

'Why are you so anxious to get rid of me?' she countered, and held up her drawing. 'How do you like this? For a George I salver our silversmith's copying, but the original chasing's practically disappeared.' So I had to postpone my exasperation and admire the vine-and-grape border, done in beautiful velvety lines on that special paper that's like translucent ivory. When she turns mischievous and amused and changes the subject like that, I know there's no use going on; it simply means I've been beaten—again.

On this evening of our dinner with Alec—he's told me to call him Alec—in the after-mellowness of good food and wine and warm companionable candlelight, he said to me with a smile, 'Your niece looks very much like you.'

'More like my elder sister,' I smiled back. 'She was the good-looking one.'

'Family resemblances are a strange thing,' he pursued, 'with apparently no limit to how long they can go on and on. There's a delightful little book by Horatia Durant called *The Somerset Sequence*. It's got a painting of the Somerset who was Lord Chamberlain to Henry VII, and a modern photograph of the 1890 Duke, a sporting old character. And those two faces, painted and photographed five centuries apart, are as identical as two faces can be. And I've never heard anyone remark on Princess Margaret's uncanny resemblance to Victoria's husband in his youth—but look at that painting of him sometime in the Coburg uniform, it's in any number of books. He was the handsomest male royalty of his day—her great-great-grandfather, but what's a century to the rhythms of evolution, anyhow? What's five centuries?'

I've always loved to hear him talk, his imagination goes off on so many attractive tangents; it's a change from my elderly clientele talking about their friends' diseases and the price of everything. We discussed the flat too—we'd shown him all over it before going out—and he agreed with us that we'd been frightfully lucky to find it, and that the place had possibilities above the average.

I'd woken up next morning with every nerve in my body wide awake, tensed with anticipation. Yet it was too early for Christabel to have gone; I forced myself to stop in bed, actually *willing* her to leave and deciding I'd pretend to be asleep if she looked in on me before leaving. I didn't want her asking what I intended to do with myself all day; I didn't want myself inventing lies about it.

She didn't look in, however, and the sound of the hall door closing shot me from under the covers like a bullet. I dressed, breakfasted, washed up, all with the same feverish rapidity, and stood at my observation-point well in advance of the front door slamming below and the appearance of Mrs. Rumbold setting out with her carrier. By the look of things she did the same household chores every day at the same hour, like most women I expect. But though I could almost depend on this ten-fifteenish exodus of hers I wasn't taking it for granted, I promise you; I'd *see* it every single day with my own eyes before embarking on my illicit activities. For anything I took I'd put back, of course, but that didn't alter the *fact*—indefensible and dangerous—of trespass.

And when I stood in the attic once more, everything was different, radically different from yesterday's stolen visit. *That* had been a sort of blind dash; *this* was planned and deliberate. I was literally drunk, lured on and on by my marvelous bit of beginner's luck. Marvelous so far as it went, I mean, but if I intended pursuing the population of the album to the point of distinct identities, and from identities to the acts of those identities, I must dig for further information; dig for it, moreover, in this mare'snest of rubbish. Not one single trunk was in evidence, which rather surprised me; hadn't the family aspired to a trip in France, so indispensably fashionable? Apparently not. And still the heaps of tatters and trash intimated their worthlessness, still the wardrobe doors hung askew and wide open, as mockingly wide as uncommunicative . . . When I essayed the closed lower door of a rickety pine wash-stand it revealed the expected bedroom utensils, nothing more. As a child I'd seen such things in my own home and in provincial hotels; the funniest thing is my remembering the trade-name on their bottoms, in a pale blue running script: *Ironstone*. Odd erratic things, memories. . . .

Well, it couldn't be more hopeless. I considered excavating once more through the mildewed mass of books in the wardrobe, and gave it up. Aimless with despair I circled the room slowly, poking feebly into infirm cardboard cartons and obtaining views of ghastly old crockery, misshapen knives and forks with yellow bone handles, the cheapest kitchen ware of long ago; sighing with defeat and peering with witless tenacity here and there, peering. . . .

And becoming aware, tardily—and only because I happened to be standing where I was—that the lefthand door of the wardrobe, hanging flush against the wall like a shutter flung wide open and its lower edge sagging almost to the floor, had something behind it. And my heart almost stopped, then began pounding: not with excitement, not with hope, only with knowledge of the crucial moment. If the sort of thing I was looking for existed at all in this overgrown dust-bin, I was about to find it. It had to be that, or nothing. And it turned out to be another carton of tin skillets and cracked plates, then once and for all we'd had it, me and my project; we were finished.

Ruthlessly I seized the drooping door, pulled—and almost dropped dead as the lower hinge let off a single vicious report, like a pistol-shot. For a long moment I stood there, my insides dissolving with fright; it'd sounded loud enough to raise the dead. Suppose by bad luck that the woman had returned already, suppose that within moments I should hear her ascending to investigate. . . . For centuries I listened and listened, craven with terror. Finally it seemed to be all right, nothing happened . . . even while I was daring to breathe again I realized how very unlikely it was that sounds up here, however loud, could be heard on the ground floor let alone the basement, which our landlady seemed mostly to inhabit. Still, the scare hadn't done me any good. On top of it, also, I realized that the wardrobe door was moving very gently toward me as both its hinges succumbed to rapine. I seized it before it could fall with a clatter—that was all I needed —and eased it solicitously to the floor like a swooning Victorian lady. And only then, straightening, could I see the space left between the wardrobe and a jog of the walk a foot away, and what had been pushed into it.

It was nothing more sensational than an old gladstone bag growing the usual dust-pelt over lumpiness, and with a good-sized rip running almost the whole length of its closing. At once—not bothering with the hasps—I fastened ruthless hands right and left of the rip and pulled it wider. I told myself the hasps were rusted solid, I wouldn't think any farther than that; if I thought I'd hesitate, dither, end by giving the whole thing up perhaps. . . . The bag was crammed full of small irregular bundles, dim and pale. I savaged the rip still wider apart; the rotten leather yielded without a sound, like wet blotting-paper.

Now this vandalism should prove to you how completely I'd lost my head. I may have intended to pry among surface objects, but not—I swear to you—not to *break into* things; not to rifle. Yet the sight of those tied-up envelopes, crowding higgledy-piggledy, seemed to obliterate everything in me but an incendiary flare of *Names!* redder than reddest neon; *names for those faces in the album.* And even while my predatory claws were withdrawing the brittle packets with tenderest care so that they shouldn't even *brush* against the sides of the gap, I was admonishing myself to put them back with even tenderer care; I realized that Mrs. Rumbold's only hope of anything valuable in the filth and dust might be the stamps on these letters. But not for stamps was I greedy of this precious hoard, not for stamps. . . . I grabbed and looted without pause, I snatched bundles off the top at random, no time for examination or selection. . . . This disturbance of the surface not only revealed more bundles beneath, but a scattering of old inkpots and pens, small debris of desks carelessly cleared out. My excitement was so intense that only belatedly I realized a cold seeping fear of knowledge also belated—that I'd lost all track of time and might have over-stayed, perhaps fatally. . . .

With the usual agonized stops and starts I got downstairs by God's grace, and safely into the flat. At once I hurried to the window. There she was, laden and coming up the walk. Let this, I thought grimly, be a lesson to me. To have taken such risks, to have cut it as fine as this. . . . My head swam at the thought of my own foolhardiness. What that woman could do to us if she caught me in the attic . . . and technically she'd be right, perfectly right. To think, only to *think* I could risk our new-found security for the sake of a crazy extravagant notion, a whim; I wasn't only reckless, I was criminally reckless.

And did I resolve to give it up then and there, my lovely jigsaw? my own private grave robbery, my very own Victorian murder? My way of giving it up was even more furtive and reprehensible than my way of beginning it.

Next day, during the usual safe hour, I made three scrambling trips to the attic, taking envelopes up and taking others down. Hastily I'd been scanning postmarks, too hastily, but I couldn't help it. Most of them came from Norfolk, which didn't help. As to dates, the pre-album ones I didn't want, only those from 1846 on, and the dates were fairly legible. You see, there was no use at all in going at this mass of letters blind; I had to have some sort of method. By selecting the letter-dates contemporary with the album-dates I could—in a sense—see what the album-inhabitants were doing at more or less the same time that the camera was viewing them. In this objective I'd no luck, in a way; the earliest postmarks so far, in the lot I'd scrumped at random, began not in '46 but in '53. Still, since it was the best that offered, better rob an envelope and begin reading, let it carry me where it would. So far, likewise, the addresses were all the same; all to just the one person.

> Mrs. J. O. Burridge,
> The Larches, Drover's Walk,
> Clapham, Surrey

My dear Sister Adelaide,
Have rec'd yr letter—and pleased to hear you

are recovered of that nasty fever that plagued you at Ransgate. Have been looking over Mamma's blue cloak, almost the fashn'ble Inkerman Blue—and the velvet still good—and think of making a Zouave from it—but shd not wish to attempt it without a pattern. Cld you my dear Sister—one day when you have got the hired carriage—get me one at Bourne & Hollingsworth's, also four yds of silk soutache braid pink or yellow, and tell me in what sum—I shall reimburse you.

Typical, the small slanting hand broken into breathless bits by dashes, the Academy-for-Young-Ladies silliness and triviality.

It is the *braid* that makes it a Zouave, without braid it is a bolero. Only I shd not wish a bolero, Spanish was all the rage when Empress Eugenie married Nap—but it is smart no longer—also a Zou is fuller than a bol and falls to a point in front—

Oh Lord; whether I groaned silently or aloud, I can't remember. Suppose all the letters were like this? In mere self-defence I began skimming till a little within the end.

My aff^ate^ regards to James and to yrself—pray remember me to Laurentia—I presume that Belle is thriving.

Yr aff^ate^ Sister,
Catherine T. Pinner

Thoughtfully I laid down Sister Catherine's profundities and, for moments, just sat. Then I discovered that my pressing intention of going straight through this first batch of letters was being brushed aside by a need still more pressing: to open the album once more on the family group now that I'd met them properly and could call them by their names. Papa is James Burridge, Mamma is Adelaide Burridge. Of the two other women, one has not been mentioned. Is *Laurentia* the Rich Widow or the Poor Spinster? Of course about Annabel, Belle for short, there's no question.

So the letter, for all its drivellings, had given me the names I longed for, or at least most of the names. And from that moment I vowed not to skim any more; who knew what important item I might be missing, what grain among the chaff? No, no; I was resolved to endure, to set my teeth and slog the desert lengths of Catherine T. Pinner, read every last word if it killed me.

Eternities later I sat back, still not released—far from it —from the concentrated crouch that hurt my neck and burned spitefully in my shoulder-blades; I'd not even noticed them till now, what with something in the letters that was growing upon me gradually—the same consistent omission that had me, by now, consistently puzzled. These particular dates, with sizable gaps between, ran from '53 to '57. And in all that time, three full years, and out of that household of five persons, only four were ever mentioned. Who was the fifth woman whose name should fill the blank? And was this blank deliberate? evidence of dislike so profound as to inhibit even conventional salutations or remembrances? And if this were so—if the letters constantly failed to supply this name—by what conceivable process of guesswork or cudgelled wits could I extort it out of nothing? Ominous indication, even so soon, that the tide was beginning to run against me . . . ?

Dispirited, I folded the first batch of spiritual lead; dogged and without hope I spread out another half-dozen beginning from their earliest date, 1857. And considering how totally my morale had foundered only moments ago, I admit it was funny—the electric speed with which the next letter brought me to life.

> I am sorry—that you shd reproach me with reserve toward Laurentia—blame me that I do not call her Laurie as in old days etc—but dear Adelaide—I *cannot*. I have no more good or sisterly feeling toward her—and never will again —it is not Xtian but I cannot help it. Think of the trouble—O horrid horrid—and we in the same house with it—young girls with husbands still to get. Think how this sort of thing cld reflect on a family—and how people wld talk—if it had got known. It did not by God's grace— no thanks to her—but one never knows. Well— it is best not spoke of—even now. I have always written her a line on her birthday and at Xmas— and more I cannot do. I only hope she is grateful to you and shews it—by learning self-control— and making herself useful—and indeed she may thank her stars that she has in you—a Friend as well as a Sister.

Now that, I don't mind telling you, administered a jolt of double realization. First of all it placed Laurentia as Poor Spinster, sister of Adelaide Burridge and the sanctimonious Mrs. Pinner. Secondly, it now seemed that the Rich Widow was the one for whom Mrs. P reserved her hostile silence. Or whether that silence were hostile or not, there was no mistaking *this* hostility, nor its target. But who could expect such hatred (for it was nothing less) to be emptied on the head of the meek unoffending dove? Hatred for the overbearing widow I could understand, but not for the pathetic old maid. . . . I'd begun shaking my head over it like a bewildered old horse.

> Indeed dear Adelaide—since you tell me that Belle is vy fond of our unfortunate sister—and even seems to *rejoice* thereat—I can only wonder at you. For a young girl to associate freely—with such an one—cannot be wise—and might hereafter frighten away eligible young men—if by evil chance it came out. *Why* shd the consequences—of her craziness—go on and on indefinitely—be visited upon you—upon me and my daughters perhaps—who knows? Against its breaking forth again—there is but one *safe* rule; *severe, unremitting* vigilance!!! Never have I spoken before in this manner—but since you see fit to reprove me with my behaviour to Laurentia—I say it now, openly.

Stunned or very nearly, transfixed by some Victorian spike of indefinite nature, I turned bemused eyes upon the object of denunication, trying to find in her any trace that would account for such aversion—to say nothing of Aunt Pinner's plain statement that her presence was dangerous to the young daughter of the house. *Her craziness*; ambiguous term to be taken literally, or otherwise? Poor thing with her flat maidenly bosom, her apologetic look, did her 'craziness' consist of being seduced with or without promise of marriage? of running off with some scoundrel à la Alfred Jingle and abandoned in mid-elopement, to be fetched back by a pursuing father? returned to the midst of her family with virginity lost or at best no longer guaranteed, shamed before them all, her prospects irretrievably done for? Nothing but sexual transgression, assuredly, could evoke from a Victorian matron so vicious a show of virtue. Yes, Laurentia's (hypothetical) immorality, if it became known, might well have cast a shade over her sisters' matrimonial chances; was this what made Mrs. Pinner's grudge so virulent . . . ? How very Dickensian it was, yet wasn't this the period of Dickens in its ripest bloom? the period of the soiled spinster become a social pariah, bearing her doom savagely or submissively? And this poor faded Laurentia, obviously, one of the submissive. . . .

Yet all at once that 'craziness' of Mrs. Pinner's seemed to glare balefully, reminding me that the other interpretation couldn't be *altogether* dismissed. I remembered the Victorian attitude toward lunacy, the casual way in which they let it live permanently in the bosom of the family. I remembered the wealthy respectable Mr. Kent getting child after child upon his hopelessly insane wife; I remembered Mary Lamb knifing her mother to death in the pleasant family kitchen, with no remembrance of it afterward. Was Laurentia another Mary, sane and frenzied by turns? Had Laurentia been released into her married sister's custody as Mary into her brother's, a sleeping menace liable to waken suddenly? And her condition, was it all or in part the thing we call nymphomania? She didn't look it, but what did that prove? Yes, Mrs. Pinner's warnings might apply as much to insanity as immorality. . . .

My loud harsh sigh woke me a little; I'd worn myself to a pulp with conjecture. Half exhausted now, torpidly I spread out the next of Mrs. Pinner's effusions. Stupefying as usual with its petty gossip going on and on and on; I was half asleep by the time I'd got to the postscript:

Tell Mrs H I desire my compliments
to her—if you wish!!!

I'd goggled at it a good three or four seconds without taking it in. Then—as violently as belatedly—it woke me up. Its oddity as a message aside, I seized on it as a first reference to the anonymous widow. I *had* to take it as that, it could be nothing else. My other impression—that there was more in it than met the eye—was strongly confirmed of those last three words, cryptic with underscoring and exclamation marks: *if you wish!!*

Absently, meanwhile, I'd glanced at my watch, and again was shocked to the marrow. Where *had* the time gone? I'd done no shopping yet and my girl needed a good dinner, her lunch amounted to nothing at all. Then and there, sternly, I laid down the law to myself: this enthralling waste of hours had to be kept within bounds. And there, tantalizing, lay the next letters that I hadn't so much as glanced at, just when I seemed to be on the trail of something promising . . . before I could weaken I'd swept the table clean and put everything away till tomorrow; it half-killed me, but I did it.

As it turned out, actually, I needn't have hurried all that much. Dinner was safely under way and the table set, then I found I'd time enough to begin working on summer bed-covers for both of us; months ago I'd got some lovely honeycomb material at John Lewis, a great bargain actually. Not that I'd the remotest interest in bed-covers but I felt that this industry, properly paraded, might ward off enquiries such as, What do you do with yourself all day, etc.

So there I was, practising deceit on Christabel and sneak-thievery on Mrs. Rumbold. I'm a fine one, you'll say?

I couldn't agree more.

My niece's mood that evening was more cheerful than usual, even jubilant.

'This place is turning out better and better,' she announced. 'Take transport, which is so frightfully important. When we lived in Chelsea the morning buses'd whizz past full up, you might wait till the sixth or seventh before you managed to squeeze into one. But here they're not packed out yet, you've a chance. I've been getting on the first bus almost constantly, or at worst the second.'

'That's certainly a point,' I agreed.

'You bet it's a point. So don't get the feeling that you're stranded in darkest Clapham,' she exhorted. 'Pop on a 137 at the Common, and you're central before you know it, Sloane Street, Knightsbridge, Piccadilly, anywhere. Have you tried it yet?'

'Well, not yet.'

'Why not?' she demanded. 'Now that you've time for it? Why not run in, have lunch at Fortnum's, do a cinema or something?'

'I shall,' I said hastily. If there was anything I didn't want to do it was waste precious time lunching out or queueing at cinemas. 'I shall.'

'When?'

'Oh, one day.' I sounded as lame as I felt; it came from her degree of insistence, undoubtedly. 'Soon.'

'But why not now? Why not take it easy before you start with Dancey's work? What,' she followed up forcibly, 'what do you do with yourself all day?'

Here it came, in the very words I'd foreseen; wasn't I glad I'd my ready answer?

'I've made a start on two new bedspreads for warmer weather.' Enthusiastically I produced my red herring. 'That soft light honeycomb cotton, you remember—'

'Oh, Lorna.' She regarded me with despair. 'I don't mean that sort of thing. The moment I turn my back you're on the treadmill again.'

'Treadmill! It's child's play.'

'But it's the same old grind at the machine. Get out and about, have a little fun, a decent *rest* for once—!'

'Darling,' I said firmly. 'As I feel now, just the thought of getting out and about exhausts me. I've got to rest in my own way, not yours.'

'Well.' She was silent a moment. 'Well, that's reasonable. Except—' a new sharpness glinted in her eyes and voice, skewerlike '—you don't *look* as though you'd been resting.'

'How do I look?' I returned warily. (I tell you, too great an affinity between people is sometimes an inconvenience.)

'Bright,' she snapped like an accusation.

'What could be better than bright?' I countered blandly.

'Not rested-bright,' she countered in turn. 'Keyed-up bright, full-of-purpose bright.—Lorna!' New suspicion galvanized her. 'If you're taking work on the sly because you're worried about money, I'll kill you with my own hands.'

'I haven't been taking work.' (A relief, to fall back on truth.) 'I give you my word of honour not.'

'But what *have* you been doing, beside bedspreads?'

Oh Lord; isn't it tiresome to be pinned down, even by love and concern?

'Well, just . . . waking up late . . . realizing the whole day's mine. To spend as I want,' I murmured. 'And no one to trespass on it.'

'*I* certainly shan't trespass,' she said hastily. 'Only I'd—' She broke off in sudden consternation. 'Oh Lorna, I've asked Ron Dancey to dinner tomorrow, it slipped my mind completely. I thought, seeing you're going to work for him, you'd better renew acquaintance.' She was apologetic. 'Do you mind?'

'Of course I don't mind.'

'But I mean, have you made other plans?'

'None at all.'

You see? Having so strenuously disclaimed plans, I couldn't very well invent pressing ones on the spur of the moment. Hoist with your own petard, I think it's called. Petard means bomb (I *think*) and for my money there's no petard like a lie.

'Well, that's lovely. I told him to roll up about seven-thirty.'

A guest, I was thinking grimly, and for dinner; a meal however simple would require more planning and more work than usual. And I *did* mind this intrusion, I minded it very much. Just another indication of how deeply my secret tunnelings had begun to engross me, and how disproportionately I resented stealing time from them and giving it to something else.

I've repeated this family interlude, for the single fact of what it displays. Perhaps you've noted that in all my answers to cross-examination, I hadn't once departed from the truth entirely? Because for some curious reason, I've a total inability to tell her a *total* lie. But—on the other hand—even if I'd acquired the album and letters by legitimate purchase, even then I couldn't have told her of my blind yet thrilling casts into dark water, my obsessed resurrections or reconstructions, whatever you like to call them. Something compelled me to keep them as secret as that extra-normal faculty of mine—about which, I repeat, she knew nothing whatever. Very few things in my life had ever evoked from me this clutching possessiveness, this unrelaxing grip of secrecy and hush. And I can't tell you why that was, either, so don't ask me.

'Have you spoken to the Black Death recently?' Christabel asked, in the course of the same evening.

'Not spoken,' I answered. 'I've seen her at a distance.'

'Congratulations. Has the daughter crossed your path yet?'

'No, I've never even seen the daughter.'

'Walk with me to the bus,' my niece proposed next morning.

Transparently this was a device for coaxing me out of the house. I didn't resist though, didn't even show my awareness of her little stratagem, just came along passively. First of all I reminded myself that having seen her on the bus, I could get my shopping over early; even with this wretched dinner on my hands I might salvage a few moments for hunting down my shadows. For I dreaded, above all, any considerable interruption such as a whole day's absence from it; the thread was too fragile, too disconnected, to bear even minor disruptions. . . .

So I came along glumly, also having to conceal my glumness; I believe this was the first time that being with Christabel wasn't an undiluted joy and solace. We'd progressed halfway down the road walking briskly in step, when an unexpected apparition dawned on me—Mrs. Rumbold herself coming toward us, and her shopping bag all bulges, too; the encounter was inevitable.

You're out early. I'd nearly said it—and nearly bit my tongue off, and just in time too; any such comment, suggesting however remotely that I kept track of her comings and goings, was undesirable.

'I'm out early,' she echoed my still-born remark, 'because I'm spending the day with a friend at Wimbledon, such a lovely house she's got and a huge garden, huge.'

The news made my heart leap, even while I assessed her unnaturally affable manner. And I understood the motives behind it, too, or at least thought I wasn't far out. In bragging about her friend's possessions she felt she was regaining the face she'd lost over our flat, but simultaneously was making overtures of a sort. A mean mixture from a mean soul; also it seemed to me that these overtures weren't unconnected with Alec Sterrett's handsome station wagon, parked in front of the house that evening he'd taken us to dinner. It's beautifully kept and extra big because he needs the space for his weekly attendance at country auctions. By the way, when he goes on these forays, it's my girl who has the whole responsibility of the shop.

At any rate we'd responded to her announcement with sycophantic smiles, and she was saying, 'So I thought I'd get my shopping over in good time,' then changed the subject with characteristic clumsiness. 'I was saying to my daughter, you ladies are so very quiet we'd hardly know there was anyone upstairs, tee-hee!'

'Oh, Mrs. Rumbold.' I leaped at the opening like a starved pike. 'I'm doing rather a lot of work (a lie) on some

94

new bedspreads, and I wondered if you found the noise of my machine an inconvenience.'

'Let's see.' She wouldn't commit herself, though obviously she *hadn't* been inconvenienced and it was clear what her answer must be; she had to sniff on all sides of the question first. 'Where've you put it, the machine?'

'In my room, the right-hand bedroom.'

'Right hand? over my daughter's bedroom, that would be.' She meant it for reassurance, but managed to make it as gauche as her friendliness. 'And she's out all day, and 'cept for tidying the first floor mornings, I'm likelier to be in the kitchen.'

'Such a lovely cozy room,' I gushed quickly; I could see her suddenly afraid she'd lost caste by the admission. 'I always think a kitchen like yours is the nicest room in the house.'

'Well, goodness knows I haven't heard your machine.' My blandishments had restored her sense of superiority; let a type like that suspect you of lessening her importance, and she's your enemy for life. 'Not a whisper.'

'I'm so glad,' I burbled. 'Because you see, I'm planning to make new curtains, also I do make quite a few of our clothes—'

'That's all right, your wall-to-wall seems to take up the sound entirely. And you're over a room that's empty all day. So just you go ahead,' she summed up. 'Use your machine all you want.'

'That's *terribly* kind of you, Mrs. Rumbold,' Christabel put in. Her voice was unnaturally sweet, the sort of voice she puts on for people she doesn't like. 'And Oh! I've been wanting to ask you. Have you any special plans for the front garden?'

'Front garden?' Again that cautious reserve, even about

the miserable patch of soil with its dying privet and half-dozen blades of grass. 'How do you mean, plans?'

'I mean, if you're too busy to bother with it just now—' Christabel has her own ways of blandishing, I promise you '—I was wondering, would you object if I put in some bulbs and a bit of grass seed, and a few little things later on? Of course I'd stop, the moment you told me to.'

'Lord, *I* shouldn't object.'

Naturally not; show me the landlord that objects to having his property improved, at no expense to himself.

'You go ahead, till I can get around to it myself.' Even to this grand concession, she had to keep strings attached, whether she 'got around to it' by doomsday or later.

'You go right ahead,' she'd repeated, and Christabel smarmed, 'Oh *thank* you! a bit of garden's so much more fun than window-boxes.—Heavens, I must skip for my bus.' She gave our landlady a false flashing smile, and me a flashing smile not false, and made off at speed. Involuntarily my glance followed her, the slim hurrying figure plainly dressed, yet even from the back its individuality and air of distinction so unmistakable. . . .

A strange little thing happened then, one of those nothings—yet a something—that's hard to put into words. I stopped looking after Christabel, and looked at Mrs. Rumbold. And felt rather than saw that she had been looking after Christabel too, and had withdrawn her gaze precisely when I'd done, and on another precise split second our eyes had met. It was in that meeting of eyes that I'd felt it—a small shock, an unformulated suspension on the threshold of something. Then she spoke, and the spell was broken.

'Good Lord! Look at me, my early start won't do me

much good if I stand here nattering, will it?' She hurried off.

And there I stood, letting what I'd seen in her eyes—or thought I'd seen—drop into abeyance before her first announcement, her intention of a whole day's absence. Exciting? Red rag to a bull wasn't in it. A whole day for illicit exploration, no need to creep about on tiptoe, no need to stand cowering, listening . . . Yes, if I tore through my shopping now and got everything under way by twelve, I'd have most of the afternoon to myself, all to myself, the precious hours I thought I'd been robbed of. . . .

I took a couple of rapid steps toward the High Street, then stopped dead; I'd come out without my shopping bag. Go back and get it, or not? As I teetered indecisively, something returned and halted me with a faint shock. Mrs. Rumbold's eyes looking after Christabel then meeting mine, those ill-wishing eyes . . . Nonsense, I snapped at myself, she's nothing but a stupid envious woman and hideously touchy with it, don't be always making something out of nothing.

While I was scurrying down the road, my vision of the empty house fought with the vision of myself loading up with wine, groceries, fruit and a chicken, and no carrier. All right, I'd buy a threepenny one at the supermarket, I'd buy two if necessary and blow the expense. Already in imagination—with dinner all organized—already I sat, palpitating, before the mystery of unfolded and unread letters. . . .

Tell Mrs H I desire my compliments to her—if you wish!!! But no more mystery about the earlier lack of allusion to her, for it turns out that she's only just now joined the household—by this letter, in 1857. And this date, meaningless to me before, lifts another meaningless date into high and dazzling relief. Isn't it strange how one single detail, previously unknown, can absolutely *flood* a picture with new significance? For now the date of the group—'63—means that the Burridge household has had six solid years of Mrs. H. No wonder she seems so solidly entrenched, so assertively in possession. . . . *Tell Mrs H I desire my compliments to her—if you wish!!*

Those exclamation points: jocular? pretending fear, as who should say, *My compliments to Mrs Medusa?* Something cryptic there certainly, or at least some sort of reserve. Will the next letters enlighten me? with such long gaps between them as there are? Nothing to do but slog away at them, slog away and hope. . . .

And discover, actually, that about one thing there can be no mistake. From the moment of Mrs. H's taking up residence, the trouble begins. Both the tone and topic of the letters change to such an extent that there's no longer any difficulty in finding and joining up the significant bits. All at once, in fact, there's too much—an embarrassment of riches.

> I am sorry that you shd find it difficult—having Mrs H with you permanently. *Between our-selves*—she is *not* an agreeable nor easy person —but since she is yr husband's sister—and living with you by his wish—you are bound to submit with a good grace—as a loving wife shd.

Storm signals immediate and unmistakable. However, my assumption—that first and worst hostilities must take place between the wife and resident sister-in-law—turns out to be not entirely correct.

You have had almost a year of Mrs H as you say—uncomfortable no doubt—but also you seem to hint that Laurentia becomes—toward her— what I can only call *aggressive?* This if true *alarms* me—I trust my impression is mistaken— that you permit such headstrong folly.

Another warning, unmistakably. And, of my two theories—Laurentia immoral, Laurentia insane—does the balance seem to waver toward the side of some mental condition, some precarious balance overturned by a breath . . . ?

Very poetic no doubt—your describing it as a sparrow flying in the face of a hawk—does this mean that you *encourage* our unfortunate sister in her deplorable manner toward Mrs H? If so I regard this as *madness* on yr part—consider what trouble L has already made—trouble enough and to spare. I will say no more except —I am dumbstruck—that she *dares* flaunt her crazy wrong-headedness—in the face of yr husband's sister—who is a rich woman to boot.

Well, well, dear Mrs. Pinner, you do become more attractive on closer acquaintance, don't you?

You say she acts thus in taking yr part—I can only compliment you on such a defender—and tell you as well that this is wicked, *wicked* nonsense. She owes *everything* to yr husband's charity—I will say no more—but you shd remind her of her position—after such a fashion as she will not *forget.*

What I admire about you, dear Mrs. Pinner, is your delicacy toward Laurentia in her dependent state, and your willingness to rub it in.

> Your indulgence toward her I do *not* understand
> —nor yr affection—which her own horrid follies
> shd at least have tempered with *severity*. Mrs H
> has *money*—and wld surely leave something to
> James for she dotes on him. A pity that this expectation shd be endangered—by such an one as
> L is—I grieve to say it but it is *so*. Also by yr
> own account—do I understand that Belle imitates Laurentia's demeanour toward Mrs H, and
> that you permit, nay seem to *applaud* it? I felt
> myself near to swooning when I read this—
> REFLECT my dear Adelaide—where this may
> lead—we have seen it at close enough quarters
> alas. I will say no more, but—

How tired I was by now, how sick and tired of this portentous reticence! Having announced fifty times that *she will say no more*, she continues saying it—yet never to the point of anything definite. Also by now, rather demoralizingly, do her allusions seem to tip the scales on the side of illicit sex? Damn the woman, what was I getting from her slipslop denunciations and tiny writing but eyestrain and headache, why could she never come out with anything clearly and plainly?

And against expectation, as I soldiered on doggedly, a thing did come through, a single thing and how could one miss it: her constant theme of *Mrs H has money, Laurentia has none. Don't let her forget she's eating the bread of charity and that she must behave humbly and gratefully. Remind her that your husband can turn her into the street*

if he so pleases . . . a paraphrase, but accurate. I don't
mean all this is new; the new thing is Mrs. Pinner's insistence, how she hammers and hammers away at the
theme. . . .

I took time off and sat still, surrounded by the utter stillness of the flat; totting up (one might put it) what the
letters had given me so far, in the way of credits and debits
both.

On the credit side it now seemed to me that I had—so to
speak—the *formations* of this petrified family group, under
the trees of over a century ago. In one camp, the husband
and the husband's wealthy widowed sister, Mrs. H; on the
other, the wife and the wife's dependent spinster sister,
Laurentia. There could be little doubt, moreover, as to
which of these opposing forces had the heavier guns. All
the time I was reading I'd had the album beside me, open
at the group, so that—constantly—I referred back and forth
from words to faces. And the oftener I did it, the more uncanny it was how those faces began taking on more and
more life and more *meaning* of their own. For example,
beside the husband's physical resemblance to his sister, it
now seemed to me very likely that he might be dominated
by the masterful arrogant woman, even cowed. And if so—
if James Burridge were that subservient to his sister—I
could be fairly sure he was letting her trample all over his
wife, in her own home. No, by the look of things, I
wouldn't give much for Mrs. Burridge's chances. . . .

I was looking at her, at the wife. Stupid her face had
seemed to me at first, perhaps merely spiritless. Now, in
fullest measure, I understood its quality as *beaten*. Six
years of Mrs. H had done for the poor woman, and little
wonder . . . now I was staring at the spinster. Here again,
family resemblance linked them together more closely than

I'd thought. The wife's surplus flesh disguised her bone structure, but the foreheads were the same when one looked, the delicately-shaped noses. Identical too their air of gentleness and refinement, making the husband and the widow seem of coarser clay than ever, and she coarser than he. . . . No wonder the two poor rabbits leaned so protectively together against the menace, no wonder the wife's hand through the spinster's arm, seeking reassurance; an automatic thing with them probably, in their pathetic ineffectual alliance. . . .

And the pretty daughter, whom one might think too young to incline actively toward one side or the other? But according to Mrs. Pinner she had taken up arms indeed, her weapons being impertinence and disrespect, cardinal offenses for the young of that day. Natural of course that she should side with Laurentia, who sided with her mother. Yet looking at the charming young creature again in the light of Mrs. Pinner's warnings, was she wilful rather than carefree? was her artless smile a bit too artless? Whether or no, however, I felt that by now I'd a pretty thorough insight on the sad but common spectacle of a chronic family dissension; that much, definitely, was to the credit side of my search. . . .

On the debit side, however, was the same irksome thing, the blank constantly repeated and constantly unfilled. *Who was Mrs. H?* In Mrs. Pinner's voluminous screeds I'd found no mention of her full name, not once. Did this mean I'd have to dig deeper into the gladstone's mouldy depths for still more of those deadly letters . . . ?

My heart fainted at the prospect; not only of its drudgery and suffocating boredom, but its probable outcome. If Mrs. P continued to be no more informative on the widow's identity—if all she could impart was her obsession with some taint in Laurentia that might besmirch her provincial respectability—then the project was doomed, it was all wasted effort and I might as well give it up. Difficult, though, not to speculate on Laurentia's trespass—apparently hushed up till now but not completely resurrection-proof, to judge by Sister Pinner's dread of the spectre. . . .

I was looking at her again, the Fallen Woman of the chaste Victorian album, for whom the rod stood forevermore in pickle. And the more I thought what her life must have been at the hands of parents, sisters, in-laws—the veiled drawing aside of skirts, the ostentatious forbearances, the everlasting penance of the outcast—the more I wondered that she'd preserved enough spirit to face up to such an opponent as Mrs. H must have been, and more power to her. But taking it all in all I should say that Laurentia, with whomever of her family she lived, would have a thin time at best. Yes, an uncommonly thin time. . . .

And all at once I came wide awake to another silence—more lethal even than the silence surrounding Mrs. H. *Where was my murder?* For believe me or not, in these fascinating pursuits of character I'd lost sight of it entirely. Now, returned to my objective with a jolt, with another jolt I realized the present status of my research. Among these five eminently respectable people, which one had in him or her the fearsome power to spill living blood, to rend life from living flesh and bone? The stodgy husband I discounted straightaway. But the consequential Mrs. H, the flattened Adelaide Burridge, the spinster Laurentia whose defiances I felt as plucky but pathetic, the saucy vivacious Belle? A strained family situation and the nervous tension it generates were present among them, certainly, but if such things resulted in murder there'd be daily massacres in half the houses in England. And ultimate violences happen, we all know this, but mostly (I venture to say) where poverty adds its daily chafing to other daily miseries. No, this background was too comfortable, the animosities too small-scale; I couldn't feel the darker, pent-up heats that end in smashed skulls or kitchen knives in someone's entrails. . . .

And also, I kept waking to new dismays every moment. Given a murder, *when* had it happened? when? Some fixed point in time one must have, mustn't one? or some approximate idea of it? But I'd none, none at all. Now I *know* that in this country places exist for every sort of record, where you can look up anything at all. Only I don't begin to know their names; and even if I found out, I'm not equipped for such activities, especially as I'd no clear starting-point. You must have *some* sort of peg to hang things on; a fact, a name, a date. I'd certainly no date, and since I'd no idea who was killed, no name. I couldn't even swear anyone *had* been killed, let alone by whom or when. So wouldn't I cut a fine figure, approaching some public archive with my enquiry?

Well! Not good, not good at all. Gloom began to pervade me, the weariness of frustration. Or perhaps my letdown was just hunger, for time had flown as usual; as it was I'd have to tear about putting the last touches to dinner, setting the table, sweeping my pilfered documents out of sight and making myself presentable. . . . As I flapped about doing ten things at once I realized that rather than anticipating the morrow—as at first—I was actually dreading it as empty, an inexorable void.

And it must have been the discouragement and discontent already in me, the conviction of defeat, that revived my weakest theory with new force. The spinster

Laurentia: was her look *too* gentle, *too* self-effacing, with an undercurrent of something unpleasantly demure, even sly? The mask of the tractable semi-lunatic who oughtn't really to be at large, capable of sly gentle mischiefs against the household peace? My impression of her had been quite otherwise, but how did one know? I was shaken with my desire to look at her again, but no time, no time. . . .

And suddenly, for all I'd thought I was done with Mary Lamb completely, she was with me again and wouldn't be driven away. Mary released, after the butchery in the kitchen, into the care of her dear gentle brother Charles; Mary living peacefully under his roof, even helping with his writing, till she felt the madness returning again, and warning him. Then he taking her back across the twilight fields to the madhouse, and both of them crying bitterly.

'Don't talk balls, *deah*, of course you can do it.'

This is a mild sample of my future employer's talk. He was *extremely* elegant, was Ronald Dancey; medium tall, slender and willowy, and foul-mouthed in his own peculiar way. I mean, the vilest words dripped out of him so gently and without emphasis that you were only shattered a moment too late, as it were, and after a while you hardly noticed what was automatic with him and meant nothing. He had a long head and flat blond hair, washy blue eyes and drooping wrists—and with all his languor I felt somehow that he was exactly as languid as a steel trap, and I shouldn't care to have it snap shut on me. His greeting as he pranced in was to crush me in an embrace—I'd never met him before—and scream, 'My *an*gel! my *res*cuer! *Who's* going to save me when Lissy the rat deserts me? *Who* do I love forever and ever?' While fracturing my ribs he'd never even put down the enormous bouquet and bottle of wine he was carrying.

From this start the evening sailed along to the point where he was commanding me not to talk balls.

'You can do it on your head,' he was saying; enormous spoonfuls of dessert never stopped him for a moment. 'I mean, don't curtains sound easier than fitting where-is-it waistlines and overblown behinds?'

'Don't be disgusting,' said Christabel.

'I can't help it, they *pursue* me. If I'm in a bus with a vacant seat alongside, and there's a big bottom aboard, sure enough it lowers itself down beside me.'

'Control yourself,' said my niece. 'Lorna wasn't brought up in the gutter like you.'

'Well, if Lorna doesn't stop yaffling that she can't do curtains—this pudding, my God, utter *bliss!*—I shall be very cross with Lorna, that's all.'

'Lorna's talking through her hat,' said Christabel. 'Just leave Lorna to me.'

Silly nonsense, but we were laughing all the time as if it were the most brilliant wit—the effect I daresay of a rather nice dinner—and the lovely bottle of Pouilly Fumé he'd brought didn't hurt the jollification, I promise you. The two of them were so gay, making such merciless fun of my doubts, that I hadn't the heart or courage to admit my real misgiving, the heaviness that lay in me cold and deep, like stone. After this I'd gone into the kitchen to make coffee. And it was then that the thing, the marvelous thing, happened as I approached the living-room door with my tray. Listeners, they say, never hear any good of themselves. . . .

'Your auntie's a poppet,' Dancey was lisping.

'Poppet isn't half of it.' Christabel's voice was so fervent that it stopped me in my tracks. 'She's marvelous. We get along like a dream, she's so—so intelligent, so sane and reasonable and full of fun. We've differences of opinion often, yes, but never a row. I can't imagine having a row with Lorna, her atomsphere's too balanced, it's . . . it's *restorative*, that's what it is.'

And I stood rooted, unable to move hand or foot. To hear yourself spoken of with love, pure unqualified love! Is it a thing so common, is it so frequent, that one can pass it off casually? I knew she was fond of me, but with a sneaking suspicion that there might be pity in it, a burdensome sense of indebtedness: *Poor old thing, I can't just walk out on her, she's a bind but after all she's done her best for me.* But no, I was hearing with my own ears that she stayed with me out of love, not obligation; I stood there letting the warmth and solace of it flow through and through me, like a hot bath on a perishing night. I wanted to rush to my bedroom, cry my heart out . . . the tray in my hands, however, was a slight obstacle. I'd just taken another step forward, when again—

'I don't expect,' her voice came meditatively, 'that my mother treated her very well.'

Once more I'd stopped dead, this time with astonishment.

'It's odd, because I don't actually remember her all that well,' she was saying. 'But what I do remember is the way she'd refer to Lorna.'

'How?'

'Oh, I don't know. Contemptuous . . . ? Well, pretty near it. Patronizing. She didn't actually say *your poor aunt Lorna*, but it was there all right—in her voice.'

'I see.' Poor Dancey, bored but having to pretend interest.

'But I often wonder what sort of fool my mother was, disparaging someone like Lorna in that way.' She was talking to herself now, not to Dancey. 'To *dare* speak so about a person of Lorna's quality. No, I expect she gave Lorna a pretty thin time.'

I retreated noiselessly to the kitchen; while the coffee was hotting up again I wiped my eyes. Quite true that my sister, in surrounding me with an atmosphere of disparagement—perhaps consciously, perhaps unconsciously —was teaching the child to look down on me; the very dog in the house knows who's despised. *I* remembered all that, yes. But who could ever dream that *she'd* remember, that little thing, that tiny little thing . . . ?

I'd picked up the tray again and started for the living-room, when again I was halted in my tracks. And by what —this time—I don't know. Some . . . reminiscence? reminder? of what? A sort of far-away echo, yet of something recently seen? recently heard? But no time to pursue the shadowy fleeting thing, no time. Not unless I wanted the coffee going cold again, and having to make a fresh lot.

'Well! that went like a bomb, didn't it?'

'Yes.'

'Couldn't have been better, actually?'

'No, I expect not.'

My leaden voice and atmosphere must have got to her then; she paused and eyed me thoughtfully before speaking again.

'Lorna, what's wrong?'

'Nothing's wrong.'

'It's not his talk, is it? That wouldn't put you off Dancey?'

'Heavens no.'

My niece had begun by lingering in the afterglow of the successful evening, and so would I have done—if the old oppression, directly the door'd closed on Dancey, hadn't begun creeping through me. I hated to spoil her pleasure, but I couldn't help it.

'Then what's the matter, Lorna? what's wrong?'

'Oh, just that old business.' Against her persistence, I'd have to admit it sooner or later. 'Using the machine on that scale, when I start working for Dancey. I don't think the Rumbold can fail to notice it.'

Christabel sat frowning at a distance and chewing a fingernail; it's part of our rapport that she never makes light of my uncertainties, but always explores them with attention and respect.

'You're over the daughter's bedroom. And the room's empty all day,' she said finally. 'Mrs. Rumbold said so herself.'

'I know. And I can practically guarantee that she's tidied it by ten-thirty at the latest and then goes shopping, I *know* all that.'

'How d'you know about the shopping?'

'I've watched her.'

'Well, there you are, I can't imagine what you're fretting about. You begin work after ten-thirty and stop at four. That would be well inside the daughter's getting home—?'

'Yes, that's how I was going to do it.'

'Then where on earth's the risk? When just this morning the woman herself said to use the machine all you liked?' She was triumphant. 'I thought she seemed rather friendly.'

'Seemed, yes.' My depression settled more obstinately.

'Don't depend on it. With a type like that it's her ill-will you can depend on, not her good will.'

'Dear me.' She was amused but perplexed. 'You sound as if you knew her well.'

I do, answered a voice inside me, not my voice; I had to take a moment to free myself from it, then another moment to ignore it.

'See here, darling,' I launched out. 'I told the woman flatly we wanted the place for living purposes only, you can't get around that. And I know conditions favour me generally, the daughter's room and so forth. All the same I'd say she's bound to notice sooner or later that my bedroom's become a workshop. She may be common but she's observant. Inquisitive too, I shouldn't wonder—given cause.'

'What cause?'

'Well, suppose she found out about it when we . . . well, happened to be on bad terms with her—'

'Lorna, now really. What bad terms? And with *her?*'

'Why not? one doesn't know. But say she did find out when she'd some grudge against us, she'd make use of it for all she was worth. And then there's the strain,' I wound up raggedly, 'of constantly . . . doing things on the sly.'

A pause stretched out.

'It seems to me,' Christabel broke it finally, 'that you're working yourself up over things that can't very well happen, seeing that our relations with the woman are entirely impersonal and we're going to keep them so. All the same—' her reflective voice became warm and concerned '—all the same, darling, I'll see. It's you that have to carry the strain of being careful all the time, and it's not natural for you. So I'll talk this over with Dancey—tell him the exact position—and see if the slimy old eel can't come up with something.'

'When he sees how complicated it all is,' I waffled feebly, 'he'll probably give it up.'

'He won't—I know how much he's counting on you. But don't you see, Lorna, it's not mass production with him, it's comparatively small stuff, individual designs. Working for him, I'll bet you won't be using the machine much more than women who're always making this and that for their families—I'll bet you.'

'One can hope, I expect.'

'Anyway—' briskly she ignored my dumps '—we've well over a month before he'll need you, let's not cross bridges. I want you to have a good long holiday, and you can't have it if you're worrying. So *stop*,' she commanded forcibly. 'Stop worrying over it.'

With total dependability, not enjoyable, next morning kept its dreary promise of the evening before. Also, in the hope of shoring up my eroded prospects, I'd changed my routine and leafed the album to its end—quickly, but making sure I hadn't missed anything of importance— without much alleviating my depression. After the central groups the spaces were once more individual size, given over mostly to the daughter. Now if you've ever had daughters, you know all about their feverish hurry to 'grow up'—the one time in the little idiots' lives when they're dying to hurry the years along instead of hold them back. Belle hadn't been different, she was in the usual rush to be a young lady and had bloomed out in elaborate dresses rather too soon, which didn't alter the fact that she got prettier and prettier. It was just at the time when the crinoline was going out and the bustle coming in, and however vulgar and ludicrous in itself, on her it was enchanting. There she stood in all the delicious knowledge of being young, lovely and in the very latest fashion, her long curls replaced by a dashing chignon topped by a tiny hat dashingly tilted over one eye. Her waist, very small, appeared smaller for the delicate swell of the bosom above and the exaggerated swell of the bustle below; her trim ankles were daringly exposed, one small foot advanced and arched coquettishly. In every one of the poses her smile—so gay, so confident—was a slap in the face of dusty Time, daring it to say she'd ever be old, undesirable or unhappy. The last pose was dated *1865*. Belle at eighteen, at most nineteen.

Touching and pensive-making, yes, but it wasn't getting me any forwarder. Inside the back cover lay—as in most such repositories—some unrelated scraps; newspaper cuttings brittle and yellow, an unsealed envelope with something in it. Merely for the sake of thoroughness I spread out the cuttings first.

> Her Majesty Queen Victoria was delivered of a Prince yesterday at Buckingham Palace. Her Majesty and His Royal Highness the Infant Prince are doing well.
>
> > Sir C. Locock,
> > Physician-Accoucheur to Her Majesty,

plus three additional signatures of eminent medical men (doubtless) in their day, with a tattered date: . . .*1 10, 1853*. Other cuttings recorded the advent of more royal babies; in those days loyal subjects did manifest their loyalty (I've also no doubt) by keeping their Sovereign's obstetrical tally. Might the envelope be more productive? Its extra size, its fine thick stationery only faintly yellowed, told in advance what the tale of its running copperplate must be:

Mr. and Mrs. James Ogle Burridge
request the Honour of your Presence
at the Marriage of their daughter
Clare Annabel
to
Horatio Billingson Swingle
at the Church of the Holy Innocents
Furness Road, Bayswater
The Wedding Breakfast to be held at
Hanniscombe's Select Parlours
Portman Square
at twelve thirty oclock
June the tenth, Eighteen Sixty Five

So pretty Belle had married; naturally, with her face and figure and the good-sized dowry she'd have. If a family tragedy had in fact occurred, one could hope she was well away from sight or hearing of the ugliness. And I was g*lad* she'd escaped, absurdly glad—

So much so that I'd actually forgotten, for the moment, my own disaster: that I'd worked this album-lode to its very end without making a vestige of progress, large or small. So *now* what, unless I could conjure up new resources? From what direction, unless from more of Mrs. P's blinding ladylike script? Paralysis gripped me at the thought. But if not Mrs. P, what else? Nothing, unmitigated emptiness . . . With a sort of vacuous reproach my eyes had wandered to the group, the motionless beings who had lured me on with their (so to speak) motionless beckoning, who had let me *appear* to catch up, *appear* to overtake them, then retreated beyond my reach with silent mocking laughter. . . .

The tapping on the door didn't make me leap *quite* out

of my skin, but came close enough. Scrabbling witlessly like a frightened animal I swept up album, letters, have I left anything else out, no, thrust them all under the studio couch. I knew of course whom it had to be; she'd come back from her shopping and I'd been too absorbed to register the fact as I usually did; it just goes to show you. I remember smoothing my dress foolishly and aimlessly as I approached the door, for form's sake asking in a calm voice, 'Who is it?' and opening only after she'd answered.

'Oh, Miss Teasdale.' The smirk on her dark reproving face was as unnatural as her tone, mincing. 'I wonder could I speak to you a minute?'

The manner of her question literally compelled me to invite her in, of course, and equally compelled me—once she was in—to ask her to sit down.

'My, what lovely flowers.' Her eyes were all over the place, as per custom, from her first step over the threshold. Christabel's gift for creating expensive effects at little cost you know already, also you know how a brilliant flower arrangement can give a fairly nice room a sort of splendour, almost. I don't say I'm sorry that the place looked especially well under the woman's scrutiny, but I wasn't glad either.

'A friend brought them,' I disclaimed modestly.

'Well yes, it's nice to know people that can afford things like that.' Having gracefully positioned us in the scrounger-class—

'Miss Teasdale,' she resumed. Her eyes stopped assessing the cost of the flowers and came back to me. 'I wonder, could I bring my daughter up to see your flat? I'd like her to see how you've fixed it up. I mean,' she appended, 'some time that's convenient, you know?'

'Why, of course,' I returned fulsomely, over a sinking

heart. 'When's it all right for your daughter? After she gets home, I expect?'

We fixed on a general time; damn her, damn her daughter, why did they have to thrust themselves upon us in this manner? Not that the reason wasn't plain as day to me, actually. Our first appearance on their horizon hadn't been impressive; Christabel and I both in worn comfortable shoes, knockabout coats, not shabby precisely but dingy. In addition there was myself, an elderly woman with that unmistakable look of lifelong hard work; I daresay she'd put us down for respectable employees in small businesses, something of that sort, and of course in the nature of things had imparted her impressions to the daughter. Then the completed flat had given her the first jolt, Alec Sterrett's car had given her a second, and little by little she'd upgraded our humble status. Now she was arranging for the daughter to look us over and confirm or reject her opinion; kind of them I'm sure, and now that we'd made a flexible arrangement for this tour of inspection, surely she'd go. . . .

But not a bit of it. She leaned a little farther back on the cushions, indicating that the business in hand was finished and we could now settle in for a nice long neighbourly chat.

'Michelle, that's my daughter, she's engaged, you know,' she vouchsafed.

Why should I know, I thought, while squealing, 'Why, how *delightful!*' in orthodox female response. All the same, I blush to admit my simultaneous pang of envy. If only I could say as much of Christabel, for all her gallant independence; if only she were loved and safe with some kind intelligent man. And call it old hat but I don't care,

I don't care. It's the crown of life when it's right, perhaps even when it's wrong. . . .

'She's an accountant, you know,' she was pursuing.

'*Is* she?' All England must know so important a fact. 'How clever she must be.'

'Oh, she's that all right. She's assistant to the gentleman that owns the business, and it's him—' she was swelling almost visibly '—it's him she's engaged to.'

I blethered appropriately, while that mincing inflection on *gentleman* gave me a new—and unexpected—understanding of the mechanisms that moved her. For, believe it or not, she was socially ambitious. And even though her ideas of society and social success might be caricatures, you'd do well not to laugh at her. For the raw place in all these muddy conceptions and aspirations was her dread of being made to feel inferior. Touch her on that spot, by accident or otherwise, and she'd be your enemy for life—and she'd powerful talent for being an enemy, make no mistake about it. Just at this moment she was working away like a beaver to establish her superiority over us. Against the fact of our nicer flat she'd placed the fact of her daughter's engagement to a prosperous *gentleman*; check and checkmate, a game that she'd force us to play in any contact we had with her. . . .

'Is your niece engaged?' she was asking.

'No,' I lilted, perhaps too gaily.

'Well, don't give up hope.' She smiled. 'Still, the good fish in the sea—you don't catch 'em that easy.' Her malicious black eyes probed to see if she'd hurt me. 'Well, thank you, Miss Teasdale—' She broke off. 'You did tell me you were Miss, not Missis?'

'Yes.' Smiling in turn, I helped her enjoy her triumph

to the uttermost. 'No one ever fell in love with me, isn't it sad?'

'Well, we can't all be lucky.' Her graciousness signaled the regaining of her ascendancy. And had I been fool enough to let this stupid vulgar woman upset me? Yes, I had been. All the same I had to maintain an unruffled civility, I had to accompany her to the door, always smiling. . . .

'Oh, Mrs. Rumbold.' It escaped me unwilled, with absolutely no previous knowledge nor intention. 'Mrs. Rumbold, who was the old lady?'

'What?' she goggled, uncomprehending. 'What old lady?'

'You did tell me, didn't you, that an old lady in her eighties had lived on here alone, till 1930—?'

'Oh, her.' She was uninterested. 'She was eighty-five, so they told me. It was her let the house go to rack and ruin, just living here in filth and cobwebs and never doing a thing about it. Then those people that got it after her, I expect they were too far along to really cope with it. So it was me had to face it.' She was vengeful. 'All that mess.'

'Yes, but I mean—who *was* she?'

Woken—as it were—from the wrongs done to her property, she blinked at me an instant before demanding, 'Now how should *I* know that?'

'Well, I only thought—the estate agent that sold it to you might have told you something, or—'

'Well, he didn't.'

'Because it's utterly fascinating, when you come to think.' The thought had taken hold of me. 'A woman who was eighty-five in 1930—think of the different world she must have lived in! The penny bus drawn by horses, and men going to business in stove-pipe hats, and the windmill still on Clapham Common, and Battersea just a tiny riverside village with a penny ferry, no bridge yet—'

'I wouldn't know,' she shrugged, as I ran out of breath. On a look of unconcealed derision for a spinster's ramblings, she'd already taken another step into the hall.

'Well, it struck me as rather an interesting problem,' I disclaimed feebly. 'That's all.'

'I'll let you know about my daughter.' Without a word of thanks or farewell, she was walking toward the stairs. 'When she can come up.'

'Do,' I said cordially to the retreating back, but my own retreat was slowed and trammeled with bewilderment. Her obvious distaste for mention of the old lady . . . and yet her decisive sheering away from it didn't suggest knowledge to me, only avoidance; as if she were making up for her first indiscretion, her allusion to the murder, by needless hugger-mugger about something unimportant, a common pattern with fools, or at least that's the impression I got from her. But then again the combination—of a (rumoured) murder and a recluse—there must be *some* connection. . . .

So, who *was* this poor old hermit who'd owned the house till as late as 1930? By her age, and by my reckoning, she *must* be in a straight line of descent from the Burridges. The dates and other circumstances fitted the daughter Belle, but she'd married and gone away, so it couldn't be Belle. Or perhaps, widowed, she'd been forced to return to her father's home because of poverty? Yet poverty to that extent, why? with the prosperous background she'd come from, and her handsome marriage-settlement to boot? Or. . . .

Small icicles suddenly crisped my spine. Could it be

that some other member of this family existed, someone kept rigorously out of sight? Oh yes, things like that are authentic Victoriana, you'll find them in any number of contemporary novels and even in one great one. The creature hidden away for various causes: deformity, epilepsy, or the thing already manifest in Laurentia, which in her was more grotesquely evident. The last of the Burridges, ironically outliving them all? the crumpled leaf hanging on till 1930? Nothing else fitted, it had to be a sister a little younger than Belle, or a little older. . . .

Mere defeated conjecture and its exhaustion brought me up hard against a worse defeat. The end: I expect those words stir, in most of us, the same melancholy, the same lethal check to the life-tempo. I couldn't deceive myself any longer; my first delusion of progress was done with, for days now I'd been treading water. All over, all, all over. Return everything to the attic, give hearty thanks that I'd been lucky enough not to be caught at my pilfering. . . .

Slowly I sat down, staring for the last time at the family group. Without reason and without hope I did it, with that obscure instinct of holding on to the last. My scrutiny was vacant and lack-lustre, as you may imagine; nothing more to be gathered from those five faces, timelessly fixed in the sunlight of a summer long gone. The photographer had been very clever in his handling of the light, I thought aimlessly; the shadow of leaves overhead made a dappling here and there, delicately, yet so as never to shadow the faces beneath. . . .

Just on the verge of entombing them by closing the album—I'd half-closed it actually—I did what I hadn't done before, and don't ask me why. I reopened it for no reason and fixed my glance on the background, which before I'd barely looked at. Backgrounds didn't count; if servants appeared they were merely part of the classic contemporary formula, designed to display and enhance the family's importance. Aside from noting (as I've said) their presence in mere respect of numbers and their being hopelessly out of focus as was usual in that period, I'd ignored them of course, being wholly engrossed with their employers.

Now, ignorant as I am of photography in a technical sense, even I realize that lenses giving equal clarity to foreground and background are a quite recent thing. So all six Burridge domestics were especially indistinct as to face, those of the gardener and his boy being no more than pale round moons. But for all this blurred quality, from among the four women on the doorstep there jumped out at you—once you'd noticed it at all—one face, or shall I say more accurately, a *quality* of face. Riveted, I stared at her. Not a child but not grown up, youngest of the four; not a proper housemaid but evidently of the extinct species called *tweeny*; no more than fifteen or sixteen, fat and ill-favoured; her broad face beneath a big limp frill, unflattering, that hid her forehead but nothing of the smile beneath it. And that smile, if you'll believe me, was more disturbing in the blurred face than in one perfectly distinct. Sly and knowing, furtive; the fuzzy outline and features couldn't lessen its horridness. *I shouldn't want you in any house of mine*, I thought. *What were you? eavesdropper? petty thief?* . . .

A movement caught the corner of my eye; glancing out the window I was treated to the sight of our landlady faring forth a second time, contrary to her custom, for she'd gone shopping in the morning as usual. Ironic, that this extra excursion meant nothing to me at all, not any more. My furtive raids were done with forever, such windfalls were wasted on me; let her stop at home all day for all I cared. Mechanically my sodden uncaring glance returned to the half-grown girl, humblest of the kitchen hierarchy; worth nothing to my project, one way or the other. . . .

It must have been creeping upon me without my knowing it; already, looking at her, it was drowning me stealthily, submerging and transforming; already my mind and my will and myself were absent from *me,* or what I thought was me. . . .

The bare corkscrew stairs I don't remember, only the grey silence and smell of dust at the top of them. I was standing in the hall, the low mean hall of the servants' sleeping-quarters. The attic door was behind me and I didn't give it a glance. On the roof began an unmistakable sound, dull but steady, as if it'd go on forever. The sky must be black overhead to make it so dark at this time of day, Mrs. R would be well and truly caught if she hadn't taken her umbrella. . . .

Standing there in the chilly dimness, the hypnotic murmuring overhead filling the silence like a swarm of bees, the thing renewed its grip on me so implacably that I'd the sense of being taken by the shoulders and pushed —literally pushed—in a new direction. Yes, and I knew by whom. The little drudge capped and aproned, long since part of the universal dust—she couldn't further my purpose, I'd thought. Nor could she, but she could *turn* it; bend it in ways I could never've guessed nor foreseen. No need either, to guess or foresee; I had only to follow. Still and silent, the four closed doors of the servants' cubicles stretched away on my left. In one of these holes she would have slept and—once out of sight of the others—pursued who knows what secret existence; up and down the narrow stairs she must have trudged many hundred times, a clumsy young girl with her dishonest look. What would this household offer her in the way of unconsidered trifles? The odd teaspoon, the pilfered ribbon or handkerchief? She looked almost too stupid to reckon herself with the savage punishments for theft. . . . Meanwhile the compulsion had begun to stir fretfully, prod at my immobility. . . . I was a chess-piece, mindless and obedient, pushed along by the thing outside myself. . . .

In a waking sleep I opened door after door, stood on thresholds, peering and yet sightless like a sleepwalker. This tranced routine left me in trance, as before. Having gone down the row and left all the doors open, aimlessly I backtracked like the Lady Ivy's ghost on its ceaseless round, yet all the while (how many beings live in us?) some other part of me woke and began to observe, even assess. The cubbyholes were almost identical in size, all of them freezing in winter and stifling in summer, no doubt; all with rusty nails or rusty nail-holes along the left-hand wall; all with infirm wash-stand-tables of the cheapest and flimsiest description. On the iron cots the split blackened pallets were overlaid with a cloudy deposit, a vague patina of decay. Each rickety stand had a cupboard below and a single drawer above with thin wire pulls hanging loose or half off. As I began pulling at them, still it was no volition of my own that moved me. Whatever thin debris I might unearth from these flimsy receptacles, what—I heard my own remote question—what did I expect to gain from it?

They weren't easy to open either, those drawers, badly made and now badly stuck. And nothing in any of them but a repellent fluff, occasionally threaded with hair. Hair, fingernails and toenails are the most immortal parts of the body, the dull undercurrent of thought that was my own reminded me. In the last room of all I must have woken up still more, at least it seemed my own characteristic impatience that made me wrench too viciously, with the result that the whole front of the drawer opened out from one corner like the cover of a book, but with a loud crack; the body of the drawer, so to speak, remained modestly in retirement. I knelt down and peered, saw nothing of course, and reluctantly reached into its murk, brushing from side to side and along its back, while hoping I wouldn't animate something with six legs or more. . . .

All that gathered ahead of my fingers was some small unpleasantness, indefinable but not alive; gritty dust and a scrattle of something that made a thin papery whisper as I pushed it along. At the limit of the drawer I scraped it out with painfullest care, laid the small heap atop the wash-stand, and stirred it with a gingerly fingertip. A single page from a book was the chief object; ragged at the edges but not crumpled, bad print on cheap paper, from which my single glance leaped like water off a red-hot surface. Victorian pornography had absolutely no limit, I've always heard, and after that one look I believed it. The rest was bits obviously torn from newspapers, preserved all these years by lying flat; folded, they'd have broken on the fold by now. The paper itself had gone brown and terribly fragile, but the print gave me no trouble at all. The room's occupant, aside from her taste for what the public prints of her day denominated 'the steaming dung-heap', had taken an avid interest in anything to do with her employers.

> The engagement is announced, and a marriage has been arranged, between Miss Clare Annabel, only daughter of Mr and Mrs James Burridge—

Only daughter: there went my theory of an invisible deformed sister. The other scraps, however, sang in a violent change of key.

A TRAGIC EVENT

> At The Larches, villa of James Burridge Esq., a respected resident of Clapham, the life of Mrs. Euphrasia Hepplewhite, widowed sister of Mr. Burridge, was suddenly terminated during an evening reception in honour of Miss Burridge's approaching marriage. A pistol in the hands of Miss Laurentia Tisdall, playfully pointed at Mrs. Hepplewhite without knowledge of its being loaded, went off by accident. The unhappy but innocent perpetrator, sister of Mrs. Burridge, was so overwhelmed by the occurrence that she instantly turned the weapon upon herself, inflicting a fatal wound from which she expired almost instantly. Mrs. Burridge is described as prostrated by grief and shock. The sympathy of all Clapham residents is expressed in the most lively manner, with the afflicted family. The sad fatality will be more fully reviewed at the Coroner's Hearing, the date and whereabouts of which are as yet unannounced.

And there it was. There, *tout simplement* as they say, was my murder.

The otherness had fallen away unnoticed, leaving in its wake a strange tiredness, a sort of collapse—not so complete, however, that a warning couldn't suddenly pierce through. I'd been up here, how long—? Dangerously long, I felt. Quickly I gathered up my frail squamous little treasure and slunk downstairs with the usual hunted precautions and breath coming short. Before descending to our own hall I paused and peered; suppose Mrs. Rumbold had come back, suppose that in this very moment she stood knocking at our door in one of her unheralded visitations and had a full view of me sneaking down from where I'd no business to be? But the coast, thank God, was clear. She might already be in the house for all I knew; the sound of the street door couldn't have reached me in the attic.

Safe in our flat, I took a moment to winnow the tiny hoard, shredding the filth into the dust-bin; of the rest, there remained only one fragment to examine, the biggest of the lot.

CLAPHAM TRAGEDY—CORONER'S HEARING

Mr Perceval Chorley, Solicitor (retd) opened the proceedings on the grievous incident of Thursday last, in the assembly room of the Drover's Arms. Mr James Burridge and household servants gave testimony. The attendance of Mrs and Miss Burridge was excused through impairment of health due to natural affliction and shock. Dr V.L. Harmon, for the family, deposed as to the nature of the injuries, in either case immediately fatal. Mr Burridge testified as to the tragedy's accidental nature, since both victims were on the friendliest terms. Miss Tisdall, having no acquaintance with firearms, was examining the weapon through mere curiosity and without knowing it was loaded. Mrs. Hopper cook also deposed as to the amicable relations subsisting between the deceased ladies so far as she had observed, as did Susan Miggs and Eliza Hopkins housemaids and Joseph Curtin gardener.

The Jury now retired to view the bodies of the deceased at Thursoe and Huggett, Undertakers of Funeral

Pomps, conveniently situated only two doors from the Arms.

The Coroner then remarked that there was little point in prolonging these painful proceedings, but seized the opportunity to warn against careless handling of rifles or lethal arms of any sort, in domestic surroundings. He then instructed the Jury to bring in a verdict of death through the visitation of God, Mrs Hepplewhite's being plainly an accident and Miss Tisdall's a painful instance of a mind overset by remorse. This verdict was duly brought in.

The Coroner desired the Jury to associate themselves with him in offering utmost commiseration to the afflicted family, which they did by unanimous and hearty consent.

Then a silence.

After that another silence, deeper and more profoundly *enclosing*, except that the rain-swarm's murmuring seemed to come through it more loudly. There's nothing so hypnotic as rain, nor so powerful in washing away the very sense of time. On a rainy day in some lonely English village, still unspoiled, you'll get it very strongly, that timelessness of rain; the feeling that this moment in which you're walking could be now or centuries ago, you can't tell which. One day in Hever, where in spring a ceaseless yet hushing wind comes across the meadows along with the far-off sound of the cuckoo, all at once I'd a powerful —yes, *powerful*—memory of Anne Boleyn. Now on my word of honour I hadn't been thinking of her at all, I didn't know she'd once lived in Hever and certainly didn't know that her parents were still there, but moments later I walked into Hever church and there they were, both of them. And their funeral brasses silent, utterly silent, about their having a daughter who'd once been Queen of England. That day had been rainy too, the gentlest, most monotonous spring rain. . . .

So: an accidental killing and a suicide. No wonder the affair had never got into the class of famous crimes or mysteries. No crime here, and even less mystery. Curious, though, that I'd been led to the answer not by the principal characters, only by a half-grown slut with depraved tastes. Lucky for me too that she'd been what she'd been and saved what she'd saved. . . . All the same, niggling dissatisfactions began driving me to a second, third, fourth rereading of the inquest, with my doubts and scepticisms thicker with every reading.

Both ladies were on the friendliest terms . . . And do you say so indeed, James Burridge? Thanks to your sister-in-law's letters I know you're lying in your teeth, hushing up something for all you're worth. *Mrs. Hopper cook* (plus housemaids and gardener) *also deposed to the amicable relations between the deceased.* . . . And what would the servants know about it, pray? above all in a period where preserving decorum before servants came next to Holy Writ? Could a little discreet prompting in the shape of bribery have entered into the picture, James Burridge? And by the way, I'd now pinned down the elusive point of *when*. The disaster had immediately preceded the wedding, so it must have happened in early June, 1865; also I'd a name for the mysterious Mrs. H. Two vexatious questions out of the way, but giving rise to a horde of others more wasplike. The accident, by newspaper accounts, had happened in the course of a large evening party. But what a *strange* time for weapons to enter the scene even as a joke, and could a joke be in more lunatic bad taste? So after all, was it just that—lunatic? The rabbit Laurentia had playfully shot the vulture Hepple-white. Had she hidden the pistol in her pretty beaded reticule and produced it on some sudden lurking crazi-ness? Had she done it like that, or how? And above all why, why, *why* . . . ?

All at once something seemed to snap in my head. You know how it is when over-concentration releases you sud-denly, and a blankness comes flooding in? That's how it was with me, I went dead on the thing in one instant, numb and *dead*. I'd thought of little else for days, I'd been obsessed, and now came utter depletion and a queer empty headache. I'd the answer to my no-murder no-mys-tery and the answer wasn't worth having, and whatever came next was probably more of the same . . . I was *through* with it, I wanted nothing but to pitch on the studio couch and sleep, sleep like the dead. . . .

It felt much later when I woke, not only rested but with a wonderful sense of release, liberation—a return from the shadows after a long, unreal interval. Yes, I felt I'd been shut away from everyday life by a smothering fog, and that at last I'd broken through it.

And high time, too.

I looked at my watch. Nearly five, soon Christabel would be home. Was it still raining? Groggily I'd moved to the window to see, when a car drove up, a gleaming car in expensive good taste. A girl got out on her side, and a man got out on his side. He brought out some parcels and the two of them started up the walk; my first sight of the daughter and (it must be) the fiancé.

There's a theory I've heard that no behaviour, however correct and formal, can disguise the fact of a man and a woman's being intimate. This perfect control may extend to their glances, but even this doesn't help. No, betrayal lies in something a thousand times more intangible than looks or gestures; it's the *atmosphere* that seems to distill between them the instant they're near each other, however careful they are. Be that as it may, there was no doubt in my mind that this man and this girl were intimate. The light was still poor though it'd almost stopped raining, and of course they were in view very briefly, but my *impression* was distinct. The girl was tall, with an excellent figure, and looked smart; her big hat kept me from getting any real idea of her face. The man was well built, well dressed, hatless. His prosperous look didn't surprise me, but something else did. They passed out of sight underneath, and then—after a few moments and a vague sound of voices—I had another surprise; the man returned alone, minus the parcels, got into his car and drove off. I'd assumed he'd go in with her, but of course there could be any number of reasons why not.

'Well,' casually I deployed my bit of gossip at dinner, 'I've seen the daughter at last.'

'Have you?' murmured Christabel.

'I mean, here we've been in the house all this time, and this is my first glimpse of her—just for a moment, coming up the walk,' I explained. 'I've seen the fiancé too, he drove her home. Have you seen him?'

'I didn't know there was a fiancé,' she returned. 'How did you know?'

'Mrs. Rumbold told me, fit to burst with it. I must say,' I reflected, 'that I wasn't prepared for the—the look of him.'

'What look?'

'Well, he's a—' Just in time I choked off *gentleman*,

not wanting to sound too miserably snobbish. '—I mean, I'd expect a man as personable as that do better than Mrs. Rumbold's daughter.'

'She's extremely good-looking,' she pointed out. 'Even if he's all that personable—?'

'Oh, he *is*.'

'Goodness, what conviction,' she teased. 'She may be so important to his business that he's anxious to marry her. Or she may be terrific in bed. Or maybe she's got him into some sort of corner, and he can't get out of marrying. Or—' she canted a sardonic eyebrow at me '—it just might be he's in love with her, have you thought of that?'

I was silenced.

'Anyway,' she pursued, 'I'll tell you one thing. You haven't met her, and I have. And under this sort of acquired manner she's got, I'd say she was terribly commonplace, and hard as nails. And also—I'll bet you anything—a ferocious climber, once she gets started. So if your personable man is all that attracted by this female dumdum bullet he's exactly right for her, and she's exactly right for him, and good luck to them both.'

Going to bed that evening I was overtaken inconsequently and idly by Christabel's speculations on the engaged couple, or rather on the relationship between them. And now that I overhauled them a bit more at length I found I'd one unexpected reservation. To the girl's advantages as enumerated by my niece—looks, business capacity, probable bedroom accomplishments—to all that I'd subscribe, yes. But that her attraction for the man could be explained in the simplest terms of all, love . . . no, I couldn't believe it; instinctively but conclusively, I couldn't. And this feeling became—the more I thought of it—stronger and stronger, as if to make up for its belatedness.

The object of discussion appeared in person a few days later, paying the threatened visit under escort of her mother. And if I'd met her a hundred times instead of that once, I couldn't tell you any more than the single impression she made on me—of understanding her own advantage so completely that it cancelled any other qualities she might have. Her figure was as good as I'd thought, spectacular in fact, and she was dressed with a sort of mass-produced good taste. Her skin was pale and very clear, her features flawlessly regular and without a trace of expression, her make-up confined to her lips and eyes, which were just dark eyes not remarkable for shape or size. She tolerated (at least that's my impression) her mother's fulsome introduction of 'my daughter Michelle', uttered a brief thanks for being allowed to see the flat, and that's almost the last I heard out of her till they went. Not loquacious by nature I didn't think her, but this present reserve I was inclined to put down as something additional. Her general manner and accent were several notches above her mother's—that was to be expected—but there are other lapses beside accent and grammar, more subtle ones, and well she knew it. Christabel'd been *so* right: she was still in the climber's stage of watching and listening, fearful of doing the wrong thing. *Cautious* is what she was, I'd swear, with that mean over-caution that marks the meaner kind of snob.

Well, we did what they'd come for, went from end to end of the flat. She seemed to take no more than a perfunctory interest, only nodding to my formulas of guidance, and paying the minimum of attention to her mother's running comment—for Mrs. Rumbold on this occasion was unwontedly chatty, to say nothing of effusive, and it took me a few seconds to define that too. She was *fawning* on her daughter, there's no other word for it; so anxious to please her that she was nervous all the time, artificial and on the stretch. Once the girl half-glanced at her when she'd made some small grammatical slip, and the poor woman flushed red as beetroot. And another time she started to address her as Millie, and almost bit her tongue out in her haste to correct herself; I'd rather suspected Michelle myself, not that it mattered in the least. What *did* matter was that this handsome icicle was the be-all and end-all of her mother's existence, her whole life and her reason for living. I'd no love for our landlady as you know, but it's painful to see anyone reduced to such subservience and getting such a meagre response. Also I was sensing, or at least suspecting, the workings of the daughter's mind: a cool assessment of the tenants, a careful upgrading . . . ?

By now we'd returned to the living-room, and a key was turning in the hall door; Christabel'd come home. She was carrying a big portfolio and looked a bit over-worked and tousled and yet—to my mind—so wonderfully vital that she turned the other girl with her smart get-up and perfect features into a shop-window mannekin. We'd scarcely said good evening when a car pulled away out-side, and Mrs. Rumbold said, 'Oh-*ho!*'

She was looking through the window after the car—Alec's of course—and repeated roguishly, 'O-*ho!*' (Why are women such fools?)

'Have you seen the flat?' my girl returned amiably, not acknowledging the coyness by so much as a flicker. 'Or is the conducted tour only just beginning?'

'Thenk you, we've seen it.' Michelle had been looking out of the window too. She quelled her parent with another glance; I felt the poor infatuated creature was in for a snubbing once they'd got downstairs. 'Thenk yo, Miss Teasdale, so very kaind of yo, it's quait chahming,' all in that very clear, slightly metallic voice. She *was* a tall girl, overtopping Christabel by at least a couple of inches.

'Did you notice?' I asked when my niece'd returned from taking off her coat. 'The girl the apple of the mother's eye and the mother cowed—completely cowed.'

'Yes, I saw, poor old heavysides. Something tells me that when her little treasure's married, the last person she'll want at her dinner table will be mummy.'

Just what I'd been thinking, precisely.

Those rare moments we've spoken of, remember? brief by their very nature but safe in the mind forever, inviolate as if sealed in crystal? Another such moment was one in the garden, if the patch of sour earth before the house can be so called. The daylight was getting very long, it wasn't quite six, the early April day had been almost summerlike, as can happen in our wayward climate. I'd brought a cushion down and was sitting on the front steps in bright sunlight, and Christabel was kneeling on a pad doing things to the border. The miserable starved privet had been rooted up—it was diseased anyway, she'd told me—and some pots of daffodils were going in, just for a quick effect at that time of year. Days ago she'd loosened up the soil and thrown on peat, which gave the packed earth a rich velvety look; from the central patch she'd also grubbed up a border of leprous bricks and put in Shady Lawn grass seed. All this mass of weighty stuff, the tools, potted plants, sack of peat, had come I needn't tell you in whose car. It was very quiet in the street as always, and neither of us had spoken for a long while; I was reading lazily and basking in between—basking in that same security of home I'd felt at our fireside on the cold rainy night of March. Sometimes, now, I close my eyes and bring it back; I can see the sunlit peace of it again, feel its gentle warmth. . . .

Its magic was shattered when the handsome car drove up with a flourish. The same two got out, the girl advancing toward the gate and the man rather seeming to linger near the car, as if he'd prefer not to come any farther. She said good evening, acknowledged the daffodils with, 'We'll be quait Bucknum Pelless gahden pahty, won't we?' and then, to my surprise, turned and said in an ultra sort of voice, 'Basil, meet Miss Teasdale and Miss Warne. Ladies, meet Mr. Manderton.' All this with such condescension it was funny. 'Our tenants,' she'd added, and it needed very little to become *our tenantry*. Meanwhile the poor man, summoned in this manner, advanced perforce, bowed and said, 'Good evening.' I rose, smiled, and sat down again. My niece looked up from her work, sat back on her heels, tossed her head to clear a lock of hair out of her eyes, and said, 'Forgive me if I don't get up, Mr. Manderton, I'm filthy.'

I can see her as she was in that moment, looking up at him with a little laugh of mere politeness; her colour was unusually vivid from fighting the unwilling soil. Have I told you, by the way, that her voice was charming and her laugh a lovely sound, delicious? As for calling herself filthy, she was quite right; she wore the same disreputable skirt and polo-neck and scuffed shoes as when we were doing the flat; across one pure young cheek-bone she'd a smudge of dirt. Yes, I keep seeing her like that. Also I knew that the Rumbold girl—beside showing off her very eligible fiancé to the manless household—had made a point of the introduction because Christabel appeared to utmost disadvantage. Or I didn't *know* perhaps, but it occurred to me strongly.

Meanwhile the girl had said in a casual yet proprietary voice, 'See you, Basil,' and the man said 'Right,' wished us good evening, and drove off. Our junior chatelaine went in and a silence fell; presently Christabel murmured, hardly turning her head, 'I see what you mean.'

'I expected you would,' I murmured back. After that, being within earshot of the Rumbold front windows, we shut up I promise you. But the nearer view of this Basil had confirmed everything I'd gathered from that first rapid glimpse of him. His pleasant looks, his unforced masculinity, his excellent unobtrusive clothes and his social ease—all of it only setting off and emphasizing the curious misfit between him and his fiancée. She was trying to live up to him, striving for a manner that wasn't natural to her. And the fact that she was working so hard at it made her failure all the more glaring. . . .

Upstairs we didn't comment further, except for Christabel's asking, 'Why in the world did she introduce us at all, do you suppose?' and my returning feebly, 'Just what I was wondering, myself.'

The unusual violence of my niece's key in the door, and her look as she whipped out of her coat and flung it on a chair, alerted me at once to trouble.

'Do you know what our young lady downstairs has come up with?' she blurted before I could ask. 'She said why didn't I collect my boy friend and she'd get hers, and the four of us would all go on the town together.'

'What did you say?'

'I said I hadn't got a boy friend, and she said flatly what about that man with the nice car, and I said he was my employer and not my boy friend, and for a moment I'll swear she was divided between calling me a poor fish and a liar.'

'Then what happened?'

'Then she said very kindly that she could hunt about and scrape up someone for me—'

'She said that?'

'She did, and Oh! if only I could have told her what she could do with her scrapings.'

'I'm glad you didn't.'

'Of course not, what do you think? Some pleasures come too expensive. I just said I was working very hard all day and studying for an examination evenings. So we parted with—you know—*some other time* and so forth, but I could tell she wasn't a bit pleased. Oh damn.' She swept up her coat and vanished in the direction of her bedroom.

I sat there, worried of course. Tolerably worried I mean, but not all that excessively. One thing seemed clear to me at once; that some small troubles terminate of themselves, while others just as small produce consequences of disproportionate size, and that this trouble was of the second kind. The girl was sure to tell her mother about the refusal, and the mother was sure to take it in the worst possible way, what with her besotted and single-minded worship of a single object; any slight upon this object, or what she conceived to be a slight, she'd resent far more than any slight on herself. A tricky situation to put it mildly, yet it seemed to me there were ways of handling it. . . .

'Lorna.' Christabel'd come back. 'Do you think I should have accepted? out of diplomacy?'

'No.'

'You *do* think so.' My 'no' had less power to convince, apparently, than her own worry. 'But don't you see? Once you've let yourself get pulled in, you've got to keep it up. We said from the beginning we mustn't get involved with those women, didn't we?'

'Oh yes.'

'And I didn't refuse, either, for the reason you're thinking.' She looked defiant and proud, not with a snob's pride. 'I don't *like* her. If she had a million, I shouldn't like her any better. If she were a duchess, I *still* shouldn't like her. Could you be friends with Mrs. Rumbold?' she challenged. 'Could you?'

'No.'

'Well, then?'

'But I've said you were right to refuse.'

'You don't mean that, you're only saying it to—'

'Darling,' I interrupted. 'You're all worked up over it, and actually it's not necessary. Just leave it to me and don't worry.'

'But—'

'Don't worry,' I repeated firmly. 'I fancy it can be smoothed over without giving offense.'

'But *how* will you—'

'Never mind how,' I smiled. She was uncertain but also relieved, and her relief enveloped me in the most wonderful glow of protectiveness; mostly I felt *I* was the protected one, let it be the other way about for a change. 'Just let me handle it.' I smiled again serenely, I was wise, all-knowing and smug; Oh, wasn't I just.

Our meeting next morning was by arrangement, *my* arrangement—which means I'd spied on the woman's morning exodus and timed myself to intercept her return.

'Oh, Mrs. Rumbold,' I plunged at once, too effusively and too precipitately, but there wasn't a moment to be lost. She looked black, already on the offensive, her ugliness held in leash but only just; no power of social dissimulation whatever.

'It was *so* kind of your daughter to ask my niece out for the evening,' I gushed, hoping I sounded less nervous than I felt. 'But I'm afraid that that sophisticated sort of party is completely over the poor child's head.'

At once it was clear—ludicrously clear—that at least I was on the right tack.

'You see,' I burbled along, 'she's reading very hard for a very specialized Civil Service examination.' This was the truth, and I'm more at my ease with truth than with lies. 'And between that and her job, she's utterly exhausted evenings.'

'Is that so,' she said impassively, not propitiated yet—not by any means—but with a slight yielding in her grimness.

'And besides, she's not used to the gay life—night clubs and late hours and so forth. I expect your daughter is, though?'

'Oh yes.' The grudging appeasement in her look and tone was less grudging. 'Michelle gets around, all right.'

'How *wonderful!*' I was smarming indecently and didn't care if I was. 'If only we could *all* be gay!'

'She doesn't miss much.' The woman's rancour was now in total surrender to complacence. 'When she's dolled up for the evening she knocks your eye out, if I do say it myself.'

'I'm sure of it—with that lovely figure, and I expect she dresses beautifully? Well—' she was nodding like an appeased china mandarin '—there you are. Christabel hasn't *really* the clothes for that sort of thing.'

'Doesn't she go out evenings?' She was condescending, thank God; I'd restored her superiority, and that was all that mattered. 'Not at all?'

'Oh yes, but just to see freinds, or maybe to professional things—dinners of the Antique Dealers' Association, rather dull things like that.'

'My, she does sound serious.'

'Yes.' Humbly I accepted the stigma. 'I'm afraid she is.'

'You'd ought to make her go out more,' she advised loftily. 'You're only young once,' and on this novel thought we parted—much more amicably, let me tell you, than when we'd met.

Christabel has dozens of friends, naturally. I know a good many of them by sight, without wanting the acquaintance to go any farther. Not because I disapprove, only because a woman of my age must be a drag on a gathering of people thirty and forty years younger, however cordially she's invited to join them. As to the nature of these friends, the worst I can say of them is that they bewilder me. You meet a young man badly needing the services of a barber, perhaps needing a bath, dressed like a freak or a beggar or both. Then out of that awful hairy face comes a charming cultivated voice, speaking very good sense. Now why does this boy, obviously gifted, perhaps handsome (there's no telling) have to get himself up in that repulsive way? And the answer if any—let me tell you—will *never* lie with the preceding generation. We older ones've lived our lives and made a mess of our world in our own way, and we can't forgive our children for wanting to make a mess in *their* way. We've little to show in the end (it seems to me) but our prejudices, and worst of all we can't get it into our heads that *we don't count;* show me one example in all history when the old have been able to stop the young. Resist or delay them, yes, hurt them tragically perhaps, but not stop them. So if I can't be enthusiastic, I feel that who am I to be disapproving? I just keep out of the way, that's all.

This doesn't mean that I don't help Christabel with her parties; when could she get things ready, being away all day? I take pleasure in helping her, the most enormous pleasure. By the time she'd got home the trolley was stacked with sandwiches under damp clothes and a huge bowl of sausage-and-potato salad; the fridge was bulging with beer and Cokes, and there'd be gallons of coffee and some extra-nice cakes. Elaborate food we couldn't afford, and certainly not whisky or gin for twenty people or more. Some guests would sometimes bring demijohns of awful red stuff, with which they seemed perfectly happy.

With my bedroom door shut, there wasn't even enough noise to keep me awake. Well, not *wide* awake. There was a continuous subdued roar—of sociability, not degraded 'party' sounds of brawls and breaking bottles; some people near us in Chelsea used to give parties like that. I know that one of the boys sang rather well to his own guitar accompaniment, I could hear him at intervals very faintly. It sounded like a thoroughly successful little house-warming and must have broken up at the usual time—between one and two presumably, though I couldn't say; I was asleep by then.

Through the lovely morning I walked leisurely toward the High Street, innocently and peacefully mulling over

Christabel's little triumph of the night before. She'd been bubbling over it at breakfast, relaying compliments and thanks to me over the food and so forth, and I was still steeping warmly in the afterglow of her pleasure as I strolled through the warm sunshine to do my shopping. . . .

'Miss Teasdale.'

The harsh voice, the roughness of its accosting—brought me out of my pleasant haze with a jump. There she stood planted foursquare, with two loaded shopping bags flanking her on either side.

'Miss Teasdale,' she rumbled on, glowering. 'I must say we didn't bargain for what was going on overhead, last night.'

'Why, Mrs. Rumbold—'

I was stupefied, *bouleversée* as the saying is; utterly unprepared for the onslaught. Then just as suddenly, I was so furious I had to take an extra-hard grip of myself. You know the scalding anger that blots out everything but the scalding retort on its way?—the last thing, under the circumstances, I could afford to indulge.

'—why, were you disturbed?' I offered a censored version. 'I'm *so* sorry.'

'Who wouldn't be disturbed, with the toilet flushin' till all hours?' she accused. 'I must say I didn't expect all-night parties, 'specially from people who're all that *serious.*'

'All night!' I ignored the sneer. 'They were all gone by two at the latest. Why, my niece wouldn't even let them leave coats in her bedroom because it's over yours, they'd to pile them up anyhow in the living-room—'

'The toilet,' she went on brandishing her earthly grievance. 'Flushing like that, we didn't either of us get a wink of—'

'Mrs. Rumbold,' I broke in, 'the party was in front of the house, and you sleep in back—'

'—and I certainly hope it's not going to happen often, we both of us—'

'But we've been here for weeks and this is the first little party we've given, and probably not another one for—'

'—need our sleep, and with the toilet—'

On her unlovely refrain we stood glaring aggressively —till all at once I came to my senses, and shut *up*. Hopeless to argue with jealous affection and blind resentment; if her daughter'd been invited, the party could have brought the roof down without a murmur on her part. And since this was the position I had to do what I'd done before—pour oil, blandish.

'Mrs. Rumbold,' I petitioned. 'I do apologize, I realize we haven't considered the lavatory, I'm most frightfully sorry. And I assure you we entertain almost never, last night we had in a few elderly friends of mine—'

If I'd let on they were all Christabel's, the fat *would* have been in the fire.

'—and some harmless respectable younger people of my niece's sort.'

'They made plenty of noise all the same,' she grunted, certainly lying; they *couldn't* have heard much of the party proper. 'For such a *respectable* lot.'

She'd given me a lead, and I jumped at it with mean alacrity. 'They may not have been the sort of wealthy crowd one could invite *your* daughter to meet,' I deprecated humbly. 'Most of them are just ordinary young people trying to make a living.'

And shameful to say, it worked. I could see it working;

so long as I buttered her up, always with the implication of our own inferior status, I couldn't fail. Mrs. Rumbold was a long way from royalty, but Disraeli's recipe still held firm. We parted in an atmosphere far less menacing than we'd begun in, and even—on her part—with dark intimations of *all right this time,* plus darker ones of *so long as it doesn't happen again.*

It was only as I was tidying up (I'd promised Christabel I'd kill her if she touched a thing) that the full realization of what had happened flooded over me—to such an extent that I began shaking all over and had to put down the glass I was washing and clutch hold of the sink for support. That woman, that vile woman, how *dared* she? with her everlasting touchiness and over-inflamed maternal instinct . . . when I thought how I'd cajoled her and crawled before her, I could have kicked myself. What had we done, actually, that we hadn't a perfect right to do? Why shouldn't Christabel give a little party if she felt so inclined? Why should the two of us go in fear and trembling and eternal propitiation? And why, *why* is the world so full of ugly petty natures always ready to strew your path with their ugly petty jealousies? Well, let that black-hearted old besom try it on again, just let her. I'd be ready for her next time, I'd . . . I'd . . .

But worse, far worse, a thought that damped my red anger to ashes, was my dread of Christabel's getting to know of the situation—in which case no power on earth could prevent her taking the woman up on it. Life had beaten me into acceptance and compromise, but not my niece, not yet. And the showdown she'd insist on precipitating might not end in our favour, not necessarily. So I could see myself constantly balanced between appeasement and deceit; a frame of mind conducive to peaceful nerves and good digestion, I don't think. Nice, and so soon after we'd moved in too; I could have sat down and wept. . . .

Now the afternoon was lying heavy upon me, the weight of idleness piled on the other weight. The party disorder hadn't amounted to much, paper plates and such. I hadn't been able to eat lunch, though actually the creature's attack had upset me less than my own furious hashing and rehashing of it. And to sit brooding on more of the same, alone in the empty flat. . . .

The street door banged beneath me, the enemy lumbered into sight carrying two fat plastic bags; obviously bound for the launderette in the High Street, a mission I hadn't seen before. The sight of her suspended both my breathing and the churning in me—only for a second though; it was purely automatic, reminiscence of the days when her departure had set me free to loot the attic. At once the small flurry subsided, once more I was in my doldrums, stuck in deep. . . .

Not so deep as I'd thought, however; within me something had revived. A premonitory pulse at first, then a thrust that set my heart knocking with realization—that the thing I'd buried forever wasn't buried deep enough, that its struggles were opening big cracks in the renunciation I'd piled on it. Also I realized that my present immobility was mere sadness and worry, that actually I could call on as much strength and alertness as ever I'd had in my life. . . .

A violent impulse nearly brought me out of my chair to dash for the attic, an equally potent reminder nailed me where I sat. What use after all, what use? By extremest effort plus a few wild guesses I'd unearthed an obscure household undeservedly stricken with senseless misfortune through a senseless agency. Who but a woman mad or half-mad would seize the occasion of a festivity for a joyful family event to go flourishing a weapon at someone with whom she'd had a few petty squabbles? A lunatic's practical joke, meant in the same spirit as a mischievous child's *Boo!* intended only to frighten—till the hideous outcome shocked her into blowing out her own brains. So at last, evidence of a tottering reason finally unseated; evidence conclusive and beyond dispute. . . .

And still the thing in some remote reach of myself fought obscurely, unceasingly, telling me . . . trying to tell . . . what? *I* couldn't help it come forward, I'd nothing to help it with. Still, one practical thought did occur to me: that through our landlady's departure I'd as good a chance as I'd ever have to restore my plunder to its native burying ground. Far from setting me in motion though the thought left me inert, reluctant, and—at the last, and after a scrabbling for alternatives—fatalistic and resigned.

In an act of valediction I opened the album to the group, more with reproach than anything else. *You've wasted my time,* I sighed inwardly, going slowly along the familiar row—then stopping for no reason, and with something like a faint shock, at the spinster. The workings of the mind colour whatever you're looking at, isn't that true? and by some unguessed working of mine the widow, the husband and the wife seemed to dim and recede, while Laurentia's face shone out—positively shone—with something in its gentleness completely *new,* something I'd not been able to see nor understand till now: the crystalline integer of the conquered self, a soul that had come to terms with her disaster and come to rest in a serenity, unembittered. . . . Of a being whose mere expression was such overwhelming proof of sense and balance, how could I have entertained the thought of madness, even for a moment? With all my heart I apologized to her, I longed to make amends for the suspicion I'd soiled her with—and that she was long vanished beyond reach of apology, long dead and silent, didn't make my desire the less; it only made it more urgent. And to do it I'd have to do what I'd shrunk from before: tunnel to the very bottom of the mephitic gladstone, read every last word of those paralytic letters, if necessary. It'd become a crusade with me, a one-woman crusade.

It still squatted in its niche like a toad in a hole, the dark bloated thing with its ruptured top brutally widened from the disemboweling I'd done upon it. At once I'd begun canvassing the least laborious means to my dedicated purpose. Take the whole thing downstairs, dust-pelt and fungoid stink and all? At least I'd have the letters conveniently to hand and needn't go risking my neck all the time on the death-trap stairs. A massive theft, bolder than my others, yet still I couldn't believe its owner would miss it, even if she'd visit the attic; actually I doubted that she'd ever seen it, half-hidden as it had been. . . .

Still debating a whole or piecemeal removal I bent, took it by the handles, cautiously began hefting it—and stopped in mid-lift, too surprised to put it down. Withered paper, decayed pens, the odd encrusted inkpot, surely these couldn't add up to that much weight? After another moment I perched the thing on a derelict chair and gingerly eased my hand into the mass, burrowing downward —and jerked back as though I'd laid hold of a torpid adder. An attic in these oldish unheated houses, after a century of bygone winters, can store up cold as piercing and perishing as a cellar's. The few mild days we'd had so far couldn't begin to take the edge from its mortal quality; I was still shaking my fingers from the dry-ice burn of it, the actual *burn* of cold . . .

Once more I reached in my hand. I shrank from the feel of it again but I couldn't help myself. Probing zigzag as before I reached it, lying on the very bottom. The rustle of disturbed letters, as I withdrew it, made me think again of something lying coiled beneath dry leaves. Beside its deathly clamminess it was sticky with old oil that clouded its metallic lustre. No antique, I hasten to assure you; no elegant duelling pistol with ivory and silver inlays by a famous maker, but certainly long out of date, a big clumsy affair made say in 1850 or '60, and amazingly heavy to hold. Ugly and sticky and cold, reptile-cold. . . . With the muzzles carefully pointed away I peered along the double barrel; loaded, at least partly.

Silence, deeper than attic-silence, took me as I stood holding it. Ignorant as I am of such things, I thought I could *place* this object in relation to the house. The she-hermit dead in 1930 would have nothing to do with it, I felt; rather I connected it with the middle-aged couple who'd had the place after her and let it go to pot till past 1960. This fire-arm plus the crammed gladstone testified how they'd made random efforts to clear out old desks, bureaux, cupboards. And at the same time that they'd stowed the gun away—as recently as that—they'd carefully oiled it against rust. For it wasn't rusty at all, it had been taken care of from the day it was new. Moreover it had the look, I can't describe it, of never having been fired at all; that subtle difference, you know, between an old object *used,* and an old one *unused?* Yet a curious trove to find in a house with a history of violent deaths, wasn't it—?

Laurentia. Once more and always, Laurentia . . . and now that I was her champion, dedicated to her sanity like a fanatic, fanatically I insisted to myself that whatever she'd done, and however incredible the desperation of her act, she'd had a *reason* for it, only . . . only what inconceivable pressures had driven this faded woman, her tranquillity attained through a great deal of suffering—what had driven her to splash another's blood and her own across that gay flowery setting of youth with its hope and happiness? what extremity of fear and hatred . . . ?

All right then, lug the bag downstairs and let Mrs. Pinner asphyxiate me in the cause of Laurentia's vindication. I hated the thing that lay sunk to its bottom, the sleeping adder, no, the sleeping Babe under the leaves—but no help for it. By now I'd taken hold of the handles, afraid of the strain I'd already put on them and apprehensive that they might tear away from the rotting fabric. And standing like that, with tension of lifting completed but not quite, it flooded through me and over me: great alternating swoops of darkness and light, and with each swoop the darkness was darker and the light was less. I was carried away, the swoon and the lifting carried me high above the body and mind that clogged the light and wouldn't let me *see* . . . and as always I didn't want it, I fought it away till the black horizon showed a wan filtering at its edges, always a sign I was coming out of it. . . .

Now before I go on, I must tell you two things. One I hadn't yet realized, and the other I couldn't know till afterward. First, these seizures were far likelier to come on me up here in this realm of tatters, than elsewhere; and second, that this present instance was the last time it happened to me, the very last time but one. But, during its final appearance, the grip of its possession was over-powering, and the power of its transformation total.

Now my head had cleared; I was left drained and listless as always, as after drugged sleep. I'd been away, how long . . . ? No knowing, these spells simply cancel time as humans measure it. All I know is that my hands remained fixed as they'd been at the moment of lifting, but my eyes began to take in what they'd been staring at for endless moments, apparently—the mat from which I'd picked up the gladstone, or what I'd taken for a mat; a fat thickness of cardboard showing a clean oblong where the bag had sat, with a furry frame of dust around it. But within this frame, a raised pattern, vague convolutions . . . ?

I loosened my grip on the handles, bent down, and with avid fingers quested along its edge. At once it yielded slightly, an upper half lifting a little, its lower half still stuck to the floor. I pried it up ruthlessly with a sound of tearing; it'd been far too big to get into the glad-stone—one of those letter-cases still used, two stiff covers opening out like a book without pages and having pockets inside for stationery and so forth; this one had been stoutly bound in cloth and ornamented with an elaborate design in braid, whose curves I'd seen indistinctly through the dust. Of its four pockets three still contained paper and envelopes, a fourth held something thick. Vandal-like I ripped it from the adhesions that held it on both sides, and brought it to the light of an alien day. A dumpy little volume with a lock, its spine pushed askew by years of the weight upon it. The same steady pressure, little by little, had forced off the tiny lock, which hung by a wisp of leather; its binding torn, naturally, through my rough handling. The pages seemed to adhere more or less solidly, but the front cover came up without resistance.

Euphrasia R. B.
Mrs. ~~George Cobbins~~ *Hepplewhite*

The victim herself; the woman killed by accident or intention . . . ?

My delirium of joy at the sight perhaps needs a word of explanation. Or if it doesn't—if you too remember the peculiar significance of the Victorian journal—I apologize. Imposed on any child of so-called 'superior' education, a daily discipline inspected by parents or governesses; kept up very often into later life and old age by mere habit; tens of thousands still existing, quite unknown till published by some descendant, and then proving to be mines of information often quite shattering, one never knows . . .

Now of course what flashed through my foolish fancy was that Alp of revelation, Queen Victoria's journal, kept without a break from the ages of ten to eighty; the most entire, quivering, living record of an extraordinary woman's life, written with her strange gift—of total disclosure and cataclysmic unreserve, untamed even by her stuffy daughter Beatrice's post-mortem censoring. So do you wonder at my delirium—till panic intervened, reminding me that I'd lost count of time, I'd over-stayed perhaps dangerously . . . I all but broke my neck getting downstairs, but my grip on the precious trove didn't weaken. Let the gladstone go hang, this could tell me more than a dozen gladstones. . . .

My concentration, once I'd got inside, became feverish.

Beneath her crossed-out married style and that of her widowhood, she'd also struck out an Edgware Road address in favour of *The Larches, Drovers Walk, Clapham, Surrey*. A thin knife seemed to ease the pages apart without difficulty. The writing would be easy to read, bold and black and angular. And just as in my original state of mystic excitement and suspense, so now in this revived one I *wouldn't* spoil it by cheating or reading in snatches, I *would* save it and go through it in order, from the first word to the last. . . .

The phone rang.

I haven't mentioned that about this time, there'd been these anonymous telephone calls. Not the obscene nor frightening kind, not by any means, just calls that attracted no more attention than others, but after a while—through their persistence, and persistent anonymity—they became noticeable. I suppose it was mere chance that so many of them came when Christabel happened to be out for the evening. The man'd never ask for Chris or Christabel, only for Miss Warne; not that that meant anything, she's more likely not to be on first-name terms with her professional contacts. I'd say she wasn't in and would he leave a message, and he'd always say no thanks, and ring off (or so it seemed to me) just a shade too hastily. The voice was pleasant, a typical educated voice with no marked characteristics whatever. All the same, when the call was repeated twice in an evening when she wasn't home, I became sure it was the same man. His refusal to leave his name I'd taken first for diffidence, then for the nervousness of an admirer not sure of his welcome, though his irreproachable politeness somehow offset the fact of his anonymity. And I *still* don't apologize for not taking particular notice, even when she had to answer evening calls much more frequently than usual; men were always ringing her, and complacently I assumed it'd always be so, she being what she was. I can't even remember, either, exactly when she'd begun showing signs of strain and harassment. Never could see farther than my nose—which was true of my whole life, not just only now.

At any rate I answered, and as usual the man asked for Miss Warne. I said she'd be home any moment now, and he rang off with his usual courteous thanks. But I'd had to glance at my watch in answering, and was scared stiff as usual. Where *had* the time got to? All I wanted now was to get the diary, journal, I still didn't know what it was, well out of sight before I heard Christabel's key in the lock. In the end I couldn't do any better than stuff it—so small a thing—in the standing workbasket that's usually beside my chair in the window. It's an original too, early nineteenth century, not a reproduction. As to who got it, and gave it to me, and copied exactly its yellow satin bag that was worn out, I leave you to guess.

'It's Alec's birthday next Wednesday.'
'Oh?'
'He's taking me to dinner and the theatre.' She said it completely without pleasure, staring out the window and worrying a thumbnail. 'Making a real do of it.'
'*We* should be making a do of it,' I suggested. 'For him.'
'He'd like it if you would, I know. Only later, darling? He's got the evening all laid on—wants to blossom out in black tie and me in Woolworth tiara, the lot.'
'Lovely!' An expensive evening out is what any woman needs, at times. 'And ask him when he'd like his birthday party here.'

'Yes, I'll do that. He's picking me up early,' she explained. 'First we're going to some private viewing at a gallery, then drinks, then theatre. We shan't be having dinner till eleven—he's booked at the Savoy.'

'A nice late evening,' I agreed warmly. 'Good for what ails you.'

She gave another of those faint mechanical smiles and said, 'Are you busy tomorrow morning?'

'Now what—' Abruptness like that, a too-sudden change of subject, wasn't like her. '—what would I be busy with?'

'Well, I could take you to see Mrs. Lisfurth in her workshop. It's all right with her, if you can manage it.'

'Oh yes!' My pleasure was immediate, but not as keen—in the face of her manner—as it might have been. 'That would be sensible.'

'You didn't think that Dancey was just going to pitch-fork you into a lot of new work without giving you some idea of it, did you?' she said in a tired voice. 'And you'll like Lissy, she's nice, and she knows the business from A to Zed.'

She rose and went out, leaving me alone with my brightened horizon—and alone also with the cold gnawing worry that spoiled the brightness. When a happy healthy young woman with congenial employment and congenial friends goes abstracted and listless all at once, a conventional mind like my own is apt to leap at the conventional explanation. In these days it seems that a single woman's pregnancy is a passing inconvenience at worst, little or no social stigma attached to it, from what one gathers from even the conservative newspapers. Still, in my obstinate outdated way, I can't regard either an abortion, or a full-time unmarried pregnancy, as a pleasure trip. On the other hand though, if my guess were wrong . . . *Darling, what is it?* I clamoured at her silently. *Tell me what the trouble is, for God's sake tell me.* I'd been on the point of blurting it before, but long habit of deferring to her—to her superiority over me—shut me up. When she was ready, she'd tell me. Or she might never be ready, and that would be that. Better leave it, much better. Trespass is such a delicate, perilous thing, and its fluid boundaries are the same for your nearest and dearest as for strangers, if not more so. All the same the thought of any considerable threat to her happiness, any weight that I think she's carrying all alone, is always enough to give me a nervous headache.

I began having one now, punctually on schedule.

And yet, next morning, I was happy. So happy I didn't mind the long bus queue, I didn't mind the grey morning with its threat of rain, I didn't mind anything. I was going to *work,* and nothing else mattered. *This* was what I'd needed, this sense of ordinary life and living people; something solid to get my teeth into after weeks of chasing shadows. Idleness *poisons* me, literally; I fill it with memories of grievance and injury and the unpleasantness of finding out—after all these years—how alive they still are, how inflamed with rancour. Standing there in the queue I took a deep breath of fresh morning air and let it out on a *Ha!* so exultant it made people glance at me. But I didn't give a hoot, I was going to *work,* I was going to make money and take away some of the burden my girl'd been carrying alone, for so long.

Mrs. Lisfurth was another bracing dose of reality; nice as Christabel had said, and absolutely expert at her trade. She encouraged me at once by saying that this sort of special work on a non-commercial scale was more apt to be done in private flats than in large workshops, and she could see I was so expert that I'd have no difficulty at all. Dancey would supply sketches and measurements, and you worked from them. She showed me some sketches, and they thrilled me. Christabel draws cleverly, she does beautiful careful designs for any period, but this man could dash down a few lines, apparently careless, and lead your imagination into theatrical *vistas*; it was the difference between a respectable talent and a distinguished flair, and some of the materials were so marvellous I couldn't wait to get my hands on them.

So the occasion couldn't have been more wildly successful—up to the moment when Mrs. Lisfurth flung the bomb that shattered my plans to dust and sent me home with the taste of ashes in my mouth.

'Christabel.'

I tackled her with it the moment she walked in; the matter was far too serious for delay. 'My working for Dancey—I'm afraid it's all off.'

'What?' She halted in surprise. 'What's this?'

'He's arranged for me to rent Mrs. Lisfurth's big machine—I'd need a big one for this sort of job.' I swallowed hard. 'I can't hope to run a thing like that and think that woman's not going to notice it.'

'Oh,' she said after a moment. 'I hadn't thought of that.'

'Nor I.' My voice came to me weighted with heart-sickness. 'So as far as that little dream's concerned, I've had it.'

'But why? you're over the daughter's room—'

'Yes, yes,' I interrupted waspishly. 'I know that, I know the woman herself's given me carte blanche, I *know* all that. And I've let myself be talked over, knowing better somehow—hoping against hope.'

She was silent.

'But this big brute of a machine is a *fact*, you can't get around it. To say nothing—' my instinct for fatality presented a new vision '—of Dancey flying in and out with materials and finished orders and so forth. If by a miracle she didn't notice the machine, she'd be bound to notice him.'

She was silent for another moment—so long that again, brushing my own worry aside, came the painful sense of her look, withdrawn and pale, somehow . . . hollow.

'Lorna darling,' she said after the pause. 'Don't just throw it overboard like that, do just give it a bash. Do, please.'

My turn for silence.

'Dancey'll work out how to be the invisible man, it's just up his street,' she continued urging. 'So don't just . . . give it up without a struggle, at least . . . try. . . .' Her voice failed suddenly, she sat down all at once as if her legs had gone from under her. And seeing her like that, bowed and silent—seeing how thin and overshadowed she'd become, my beautiful happy girl—I couldn't bear it a moment longer.

'Christabel darling,' I entreated. 'Christabel. Oh please, *please*.'

At least she wasn't running from me, shutting herself in and shutting me out. Whether she was taking pity on me, or whether she'd got to the point where she couldn't endure it alone any longer, I don't know. Whatever the reason at any rate, she answered almost at once and unresistingly.

'It's—it's that—' she said in a dead voice. '—Basil Manderton.'

I gaped; the name meant nothing to me whatever.

'You saw him,' she laboured on. 'With the—with that girl. Downstairs.'

My protecting blankness clung a moment, then exploded about me in fragments like a house under a direct hit. After a moment I barely managed to whisper, 'My God.'

'Yes,' she assented. 'Oh yes.'

Silence spread out like dark water; in its depth and chill I was seeing, numbly, vague shapes of portent and consequence. . . .

'He—he must have been waiting near the bus stop, the first time,' she was saying in that plodding, labouring voice. 'His car came abreast as soon as I'd turned into our road, and he—he got out and—'

She stopped; I was still too pole-axed to urge her on.

'I didn't even recognize him for an instant,' she pursued haltingly. 'And when I did I was furious—I was as off-putting as I could be, straightaway. All I could think of was the trouble he'd be making for us—and *what* trouble—!'

'And then?' I ventured; she'd made another long pause.

'He waited again. And again, and again. He'd ask me—beg me—just to talk to him. And so respectful and so sad with it, so . . . heart-broken.' She laughed harshly. 'He does it very well, the heart-broken bit.'

'But that girl downstairs—' by now I'd got hold of my whirling wits '—she's *engaged* to him!'

'She's not,' Christabel contradicted. 'He swears she's not. He's been sleeping with her for a long time, of course—' a constriction spoiled her lovely mouth '—and there's absolutely no more to it than that.'

'Oh.'

157

'So he simply wore me down into meeting him—once—for a drink, and other times we've met and just talked. He's—he's frightfully attractive, you know.'

I did know; just from that first glance at him from our window, I'd known. This man's quality could do what Alec's steady, sober charm could never do—topple the most level-headed girl into reckless abandonment, wildness. . . .

'Does he want to marry you?'

'Marry!' She laughed again. 'Lorna darling, don't be naïve.'

'I expect the girl's important to him in a—' I was trying to repair my clumsiness '—in a business way.'

'Yes, she is, she knows the ins and outs of his office thoroughly. He says that's the only reason the affair's gone on so long.'

'He's used her and he's ready to drop her.'

'Yes.' She had only just kept from wincing.

'And she won't agree to be dropped easily—not by the look of her.'

'That's the least of his worries.' Again that alien grating sound that wasn't a laugh. 'He says she's good but she thinks she's indispensable, and she's not. And he says he's got a man accountant who wants to come in with him as a partner, and he'd prefer that.'

'I see.'

'Also he says he's given up seeing her, almost from the day he'd met me. Whether or not I'm fool enough to believe him, isn't the point.' Her smile was desolation itself. 'He says he's ready to tell her they're through, any day. And he's fairly certain she'll walk out, and he says so much the better.'

'You mean that's how he *hopes* she'll take it.'

'And he makes no bones about having slept with her.' She'd ignored my raven-croak deliberately. 'He says any single man and most married men will have a tumble with any good-looking girl from staff, above all when the girl's made it clear—from the beginning—that she's all for it.'

Emotions at bursting point are said (I believe) to produce the flattest banalities. So now I got up, murmuring witlessly, 'I'd better see about dinner, hadn't I.'

'That—that engagement.' I'd had to come back to it; it stuck in my throat. 'There must be *some* foundation for the mother's being so definite about it.'

'That, yes,' she murmured. Her dinner had gone almost untouched, she wouldn't have dessert, and now sat with coffee before her, untasted; every now and again she'd spoon up a few drops and let them dribble back. 'I made rather a point of that, myself.'

'And?'

'Well, first he said he wasn't responsible for other people's brainstorms. Angry, you know, sulky. Then he said it probably stemmed from her position in the office, her idea of her own importance. He thinks she's begun to consider herself a sort of partner, actually.'

'So that's his explanation.' Into her long pause, I'd finally ventured a trifle of irony. 'Do you believe it?'

'Yes, I believe that's part of it. My own idea is—' she reflected, frowning a little '—that the girl fed her mother this engagement yarn as a cover-up for her weekends with him—weekends and longer—'

'Don't tell me,' I offered sardonically, 'that the mother'd object to her daughter's affair with a *prosperous* man.'

'Yes—and no,' she returned. 'For conventional moral reasons, of course, she wouldn't object. But if she thought the girl'd get nothing out of it in the end—no marriage, nothing solid in the way of money—she might cut up rough enough to be a nuisance. But going off on holiday with a fiancé, that would make it all right. Anyway,' she smiled faintly, 'the old girl's so besotted over her that if a duke wanted to marry her little darling, she'd see nothing out of the way in it.'

'So you think the engagement's just the girl's lie,' I summed up. 'Out of whole cloth.'

'Not exactly—I don't think it's quite that simple. I'd guess it *began* as a lie—a handy excuse—and got to be a settled idea with the mother. And by then, maybe, the girl hadn't the nerve to contradict it, or just wanted to keep things peaceful. Or maybe she'd just got in the way of taking it for granted herself—just assuming it.'

'But that man.' I was incredulous. 'Hasn't he known all along what her expectations are?'

'He's known, all right.'

'But surely—surely he wouldn't just let her go on blindly like that, hoping?'

'It's just what he would do, you know.' Her smile, for all its faintness, was dark and grim. 'He'd let her go on thinking what she liked, for as long as he found it convenient. Then when it wasn't convenient any more—the chop. With no warning at all, either.'

'But that's cold-blooded—inhuman.' I was genuinely aghast. 'The girl's not a pleasant person, granted, but she's got feelings like anyone else, she can feel disappointment and misery and humiliation like anyone else—'

'That's the least of his worries,' she returned stonily. 'He's kept putting off the showdown—he says—because he couldn't have replaced her at once if she'd walked out.

But now he can replace her, so she's welcome to go when she likes.'

A long time passed—or seemed to pass—before I murmured, 'What will you do?'

'Oh God, how do I know?'

An affair? I asked silently. *Get it out of your system?*

'And if you think an affair would get it out of my system—'

I've told you how often this happened between us—this replying to unspoken thoughts.

'—it won't. He'll use me like that girl—for as long as he's inclined, and no longer. I can't waste a few years of my life getting over him, I—I—'

She groped painfully; I waited.

'—I've never felt anything remotely like this—for anyone. Not ever, before. It can cripple me for . . . for longer than I can afford. So an affair—then a gay brushing-off—*no*. That is, if I can hold out against him. If I can stand it.' She rocked herself a little. 'If, if, if.'

And I saw what she was doing: steeling herself to endure. A sight like that is no fun at all, even with someone you don't know.

'He says he's given up sleeping with her, almost from the day we met. Whether I'm fool enough to believe him, isn't the point.' Her smile was ghastly. 'And just as you said, she's not making it easy for him. Not a bit easy. I'd have thought,' she sighed, 'that the thought of his being —her lover—would have put me off, as a matter of pride. It hasn't done though,' her dead voice laboured on. 'I have no pride.'

Brought low, was all I could think, *my Christabel with her loveliness, her intelligence, all brought low by a man like that.* She looked beaten, yes, *beaten,* and my heart contracted with such pain—and fear—that I can't begin to describe it.

'Sorry, Lorna.' She'd returned from far away. 'I wasn't going to bother you with this. Now about this machine complication, I'll see Dancey tomorrow and—'

'You'll do nothing of the sort, I'll see him myself.' Mere love and foreboding made me snap at her. 'I've a tongue in my head, I hope—' Belated shock lanced me awake to something new. 'Christabel! if those two downstairs find out—if one of them sees you with him—'

'They won't,' she snapped in turn. 'Basil's no more anxious for unnecessary trouble than we are. What did you think?'

Life went on. Imbecile expression; what else can it do? A monster arrived one day, displacing my little machine from its table and looking twice as huge and ominous as I remembered it.

'Too much noise? *Balls*, deah,' said Dancey, who'd brought it. 'The difference between this and your little one is so twee that your old fart downstairs can't possibly notice it—unless she squats underneath you all day, listening.'

'Well, if you think so . . . but Ronald, if the woman sees you dashing in and out with those big bolts of material—'

'See me? she?' His contempt was limp but final. 'If I can't run rings around that two-stroke rump, it's too bad. She goes out mornings, you said? just when?'

So we fixed up signals, to be made from my window.

'I'll loiter palely outside like that damned fool in the swamp or something,' he explained, 'till you give me the all-clear.'

He was revelling in the stealth and furtiveness of it, just as Christabel'd said.

'You're dated up with Lissy for another couple of weeks?' he asked in departing. 'So by then I'll have sketches and all, and you're *in* it to the eyeballs, deah.' He gave me the evillest grin. 'Hist hist, so saying he pissed—off.'

All the same I circled the new arrival once or twice, like a hunter stalking its prey; my God, it did look big. With misgiving I connected and ran it for a good few moments. Actually the increase of noise was slight, just as he'd said, but the vibration . . . I *felt* rather than heard it as powerful. In less than no time I was charging down the street like the Light Brigade, and returned via taxi with a square of cork matting and another square of thick carpet, a remnant. And after I'd lifted a ton of machine and got them under the table and lifted the ton back with pantings and strainings, and ran it a full minute or more—only then was I satisfied. The extra thickness beneath seemed to swallow its heavy pulsing to such an extent that only the closest and most continuous listening (I felt) could catch it. The sight of it of course, its size, would give me away at once as being commercially employed. But from the danger of prying eyes I was safe, thank God, and even bragged mildly to Christabel about having arranged it all myself. And she gave me that new smile of hers, always faint and pale nowadays, that made my heart ache.

Still, her own life—always a busy one—was going on too. She was having half a dozen older friends to dinner next week, people associated with art in one way or another, and from those I don't retreat as from her younger lot; I can't contribute anything to their talk but I'm grateful to hear it, and grateful that such people exist. Alec was coming too, I was glad of that. For all my feeling of gathering complexities, the thought of doing them a lovely dinner was a cheerful thought.

All during this time she'd be out very late, a good many nights in the week. I don't know what was happening, I didn't want to know and still don't know. The thought of the man wasn't pleasant, and it was none of my affair; if love is your sickness it's *your* resources of body and mind that have to cope with it, not someone's else. My chief comfort—foolishly enough—was thinking that at least I'd stopped being the eternal weak reed to the wage earner. It wasn't much, but it gave enough lift to my spirits that might otherwise have settled into constant depression, foreboding and God knows what; you must have *something* from which you draw courage.

I even found energy enough—when I'd remembered it —to excavate Mrs. Hepplewhite's journal—on a note of postponed and rising excitement at that. True that my fierce original zest for the search was dulled, true that the inhabitants of the album—even poor Laurentia whom I'd longed to protect—were dim and receding. But I'd had no chance as yet to look at this latest find, which *might* answer the question that still dogged and haunted me, the *why* of the gentle spinster's guilt for two deaths. Or if it didn't, then name it at its lowest terms, curiosity reviving, and pretty strongly too.

And so: you remember my rosy hopes, my childlike faith in Victorian journals as shedders of light, as guiding threads into the secret byways of life? Within ten minutes and as many pages, it was all dust and ashes. First of all the thing seemed principally, to my disgust, a small account-book. Sums crowded sums, addition and subtraction overflowed into the margins. This arithmetic consistently involved comfortable amounts of money, in a sort of middle-class range. Here and there were remarks and interjections but plainly casual, not meant for any unburdening of the soul. And when they began to be more numerous I could heartily wish they hadn't been, for I could have done without their message—uniform as a desert and as barren, no less in fact than a death-blow.

Before me stood a mean, common woman with a mean, common soul. Her every action or activity, her family and her comings and goings, represented themselves to her not in terms of pleasure or concern or interest, only of expense. The entries were at least meticulously dated, but that wasn't enough. As I plodded on, the extraordinary number of multiplications by three seemed to indicate sizable holdings in the financial Gibraltar of the period, reverently referred to by Dickens and Thackeray and lesser novelists as the Three Percent Consols. In this solid jungle of arithmetic stray sentences appeared—jottings more accurately, yet their skimpiness had a narrative power of its own.

Cabbages!

Cryptic notation standing alone and repeated at intervals. After these, a positive burst of eloquence: *Went into kitchen garden and counted.* More sums, then all but a three-volume novel.

> Took gardener in act, 2 cabbages under coat. Had to dismiss him myself, Thomas refused, weakly. Thieving wretch, shd be in gaol with family starving. Thomas wd not consent. Spineless as usual.

The next battle-cry is *Tea-leaves!* clarified by later entries.

Servants nowadays. Object to drying tea-leaves for a second use. Fine ladies indeed, lazy idle sluts. Told cook, Streets and workhouses full of your kind, join them if you wish. She is stopping of course. That kind easily brought to heel—

—and more and more of the same thing, as far as I went the first time. You'd think it would embarrass a woman, wouldn't you, to see her own ugly soul so nakedly exposed by her own words? Not this woman, though. Half-buried among her figures for 1856, the unimportant fact that her husband has died. *Must think what to do with house, much too big for me now. Cost of funeral exorbitant and did not scruple to say as much to the Furnisher.*

A last tear for her husband's grave; I felt I'd had enough of her style for one day.

The next event, unpredictable—fatality always is—was the moment next evening when our landlady was hauling back two bloated bags of laundry, and Alec had just picked up Christabel for his birthday binge. She'd set down a bag in order to open the gate when here the two of them were, coming down the walk. My girl hadn't bought clothes for a long time, of that I was certain; she hadn't a rag on, this evening, that wasn't a couple of years old and older. Her elegant gown of stiff almond green satin she'd got at a sale, ages ago; her cape, three thick fox-skins of a soft even tan, mounted on pale-gold satin, I'd given her for a birthday long past. And saved for a year to get it too, and not on the never-never; I wouldn't have anything on her back that wasn't paid for. She had on green satin slippers with twinkles on the toes, and pale beige satin gloves. For all her far-from-new finery she shimmered in that dingy street like a bird of paradise, and with like vividness it smote me that my brilliant inspiration—to represent her as a dowdy book-worm with dowdy friends and ditto clothes—hadn't been so brilliant after all. Oh what cruel cruel luck, that she'd had to run into the woman at just this moment, Oh dear Oh dear. . . .

The mere sight had driven me instinctively a couple of steps back from the window, to where I could just see by craning. Christabel had nodded, and Alec raised his soft black hat that made him look so distinguished, and black tie didn't set him off badly either, I promise you. And the woman—will you believe it—turned full around and stared after them, just right-about-faced and stared undisguisedly. They got into the car and drove off, and still she stood there another long moment, looking after them. Then she turned once more, slowly, and directed a look at our windows, one single look; I'm glad I wasn't standing there in view, to get the full blast of it. You could *see* her remembering Christabel's refusal to 'go on the town' with her daughter, you could *see* her registering—even her thick wits—the blatancy of my lies and the purpose of them, and the slight that had been put on her darling child. Not that I blamed her, haven't I a darling child myself? But if only I hadn't piled it on to quite such an extent; if only, only . . .

She and her bags had vanished; slowly I sat down, to plumb the depths of this latest catastrophe. *Now you're for it,* a pale voice was whispering in my ear, *now you're well and truly for it,* and with all my heart (plus the bonus of a cold shiver) I agreed. Now as never before the woman would be on the watch—for any ghost of reason for complaint, for any pretext however trivial—and she'd use it against us to the utmost. A sort of undeveloped stroke went off in my head; from it I emerged with two iron resolves. First, I'd *still* keep this from Christabel as long as possible, I'd die before I added to the weight she was already carrying. Second, from now on I'd walk on eggs, I'd take the most deathly care not to give a shadow of offence that she could act on—delightful prospect in itself. If only I had Dancey's work to distract me now, if only it were immediate instead of in prospect. . . .

Considering this latest blow added to my current oppressions, you may be surprised to find me toying with Mrs. Hepplewhite's journal again; I was surprised myself. One reason was our little dinner-party of the night before, and its going off so well it'd given my spirits the lift that unimportant things—you know?—often do. Then again the same old problem, nothing to do after I'd washed up and set the place to rights; no resource but this laboured, lacklustre scrutiny.

> Have suggested to James that I move in with him, share household expense. He shd welcome it, saddled as he is with a lot of useless women. James said Adelaide unwilling, her insolence. Reasoned with him, my wiser counsels prevailed.

Well! that woke me up a bit, I admit. The longest entry so far, and the date September 1857. So here she is, the rich widow, ensconced in this very house.

> The kitchen needlessly profuse, a sinful waste. Offered Adelaide my good offices to set matters right. She refused, not amiably. That pauper sister of hers, a needless mouth filling itself daily at my brother's expense. Poor James, lucky for

him that at last someone is in this house to take his part.

Instant meddling, true to type. Naturally the sight of Laurentia getting food and shelter without scrubbing floors ten hours a day would madden her beyond endurance.

> Have only just learned old maid turned out of room that now is mine, and lodged in smaller one. Quite good enough, too good in fact. Eats of my brother's substance and does nothing but some sewing and mending that any upstairs maid cld do better.

Yes, for the moment she's set foot in the house, the purpose of her campaign is clear—to get Laurentia thrown out.

> Have put to James, squarely, the matter of this parasite. He shuffles and evades as usual, says he can well afford. Weak, like Thomas. If he has got no resolve I must have it for *both*, it is my *duty*—

The tap on the door sent a cruel stab all through me and made me leap with its sharp demand; it could be only one person, the last one in all the world I wanted to see.

If my allusions to the ogress have been scarce of late, it's not because she wasn't constantly on my mind. I'd seen her outside on various occasions, always (thank God) at a distance, yet even so her look was enough to tell me all. Her daughter had been jilted and she was taking it hard, I knew just how hard; her emotional state was as clear to me as a map. She'd bragged to all and sundry as she'd bragged to me, she'd enlarged far and wide on Michelle's brilliant prospects, and here it was, all gone bitter and bad. Even in walking she seemed to give off a sort of *murk* that made her actually alarming, and my anxiety to avoid her soon produced an equal skill at the exercise. In truth, what I felt for her was pity—as much as I could spare from our own entanglements. Sometimes at night, when I'd lie awake and hear my girl's wakefulness on the other side of the wall, it would seem to me that our misery was darkly reflected on the floor below, like an image in one of those blotched perished old mirrors. And Oh God, if ever it dawned on the woman who was responsible for stealing her daughter's future husband, for of course that's how she'd put it to herself. . . .

'Miss Teasdale!' she hissed at me the moment I'd opened. 'If you'd *kindly* tell Miss Warne t'ask her visitors to go downstairs a little quieter, when they're leaving—!'

Having shot her bolt she lumbered about and moved toward the stairs. Obviously she'd thought, mind you, that I'd let such an observation pass—in which she was making the mistake of her life.

'Mrs. Rumbold!'

She stopped because the quality of my voice stopped her, whether she would or no. True that I'd resolved to walk softly, to preserve the peace at all costs, but the lowliest worm has limits.

'What,' I demanded, 'what are you talking about?'

'You should know,' she snarled. Her back was half toward me, but already I'd the impression she was drawing in her horns.

'You mean the few friends we had to dinner last night?'
I pursued. 'You mean *that?*'

'Well yes, clatterin' down those bare steps fit to wake
the dead—can't even get my sleep, with everything else
I've got on my plate—!'

'The steps are bare because you've left them bare,' I
pointed out venomously. 'It *is* your place to carpet them,
I believe? This *is* your house, after all?'

She was already plunging downward in undisguised
rout, and I pointed up my victory by going in and slamming the door as hard as I could. All the same, through
my considerable moral uplift, ran that resistant vein of
pity and comprehension. Helpless love and helpless outrage at the injury inflicted on her child had come to a
boil in her and foamed over; she'd *had* to take it on something or someone, and we were nearest at hand. No, her
defeat gave me no pleasure, only an added cheerlessness.
Mechanically, meanwhile, I'd crawled back to the journal
merely because I'd been interrupted while reading it; a
resumption sad, spiritless and divested of even the faint
interest I'd had before. Still, it was borne in on me that
the arithmetic grew less and the written entries much
longer—undoubtedly because she'd new spites to divert
her from her former sole preoccupation. Also, by implication of what followed, I gathered that her attack on
Laurentia had been repulsed, and her energies concen-
trated on a new target.

> Adelaide hires the carriage too frequently, thinks
> herself a duchess instead of a tradesman's wife
> I fancy—

Yes, I was right. Adelaide will not change her regular
butcher for one who charges a few farthings less, Adelaide

has paid *15 shillings!!* for a pineapple. But the real grievance is the carriage.

> Never invites me, goes off with the daughter
> and beggarwoman. I say pointedly I wld find it
> convenient to go likewise. A. opens her eyes wide
> and says, But Euphrasia, I wld not venture to
> ask a lady of your means into a hired carriage.
> The pauper put her up to say that I'll swear, not
> brains enough to think of it herself. As for my
> means, what affair of hers? Insolence. NOTE
> THIS.

Sinister rather, the capital letters? Also her venom's adaptable, frustrated in one direction it'll find another; of hatred she has enough and to spare, for all. And also, by mere instinct, I feel that her seemingly abandoned spites are only laid by for the moment, to wait on a more propitious season; a great bider of her time, Euphrasia strikes me as being.

> Belle shockingly spoiled. Both women to blame,
> Adelaide doting, old maid as indulgent as
> mother and worse. The child will grow up a
> bold forward miss whom no man will marry if
> not taken in hand. A smart touch of the rod wld
> subdue and amend but shd be done *promptly*.

So now Belle's the target. And by the way—spurred by this family contention, I imagine—her writings begin to swamp her figures and even to display something, for her, very like eloquence.

> Belle sometimes so pert that I itch to leave the
> mark of my fingers on her face. Let her go on
> thus and they will never find a husband for her

for twice her dowry, wch I suppose is generous. Another old maid on their hands, I shd laugh if it were so. Nasty chit, and has another new frock, best French muslin and real Honiton lace, *ridiculous*. No child of mine ever *dared* look or speak so to me; I knew too well how to correct it.

I don't doubt it for a moment, dear Euphrasia, and your scanty reference to your own children bears out your own witness. *Sophia's birthday. Nuisance, but suppose I shall have to send something—*

Now just here, doubts began to creep in. For all my virtual abandonment of the quest, unconsciously I'd never stopped watching and sniffing after some lethal trace, anything of dimension *sufficient* to justify what happened. For it did happen; that much is undeniable. Now if only my gentle spinster had kept a journal, instead of this sordid woman; what might not have been revealed, what insult added to injury, what inner turmoil mounting up and up to some last pressure, unbearable.

Belle provoking beyond endurance, slapped her; Adelaide exclaims, pauper rushes at me, *dares* to push my hand away. I observe to A. that the girl has something to lose by offending me; pauper takes it on herself to answer, "She wants or needs nothing of yours." Ignoring her, as I walk out I tell Adelaide, "Bethink yourself that your daughter may be the loser, through this madwoman's antics." A smart hit, I flatter myself; let them digest it.

Unpleasant to be sure, but still a long way from explaining two women violently dead within seconds. No, still no adequate pointer to such a cataclysm, not nearly adequate.

> Horrid chit has got herself engaged. How she has caught the Swingle boy of all people is beyond me, a family as rich as they, James is nothing beside them. He was tricked into it somehow I doubt not, or her face has done it for her, beauty is vain but men are *fools!!!*

Three exclamation points, bitterness can't go farther. Of course Belle's good fortune is old news, but now my pleasure is all in dwelling—in *gloating*—over the way Euphrasia's taking it. For it's killing her; it's eating to her very soul, she can't bear it. Especially after her dire prophecies of withered spinsterhood for Belle—and here the saucy miss has won what's obviously the prize catch of her circle.

> Adelaide and that other one beside themselves with joy, it turns my stomach to see them. The three of them forever off in carriage, spending my brother's money like water. Seamstress in house all day, white satin for bridal gown £2 *the yard*, madness. Oh if I could see those puffed-up women brought low, Oh if they cld learn that pride goeth before a fall. I wld give a tidy sum to see it and never grudge the expense, be it shillings or *sovereigns*—

Oh Lord! I couldn't go on, it was like having black acrid smoke in your eyes. But as I slapped the ragged covers shut and slapped the workbox lid smartly upon it, I realized something. Reading about love doesn't tire you, it warms and restores you. But reading about hate, you can only stand a certain amount of it, it wears you out. Actually it wasn't my eyes that felt raw with the rancid fume of Euphrasia's ill-wishing, it was all of me that was raw—weary—with disgust.

Still, before giving it up for that day, I did what I'd never done before—riffled the book to its very end—and made two minor discoveries. First, she hadn't used it all up, there were lots of blank pages at the end. Second— and much more intriguing—she'd made her last entry on June 10, the day before the wedding. This date was the one thing I'd sneaked a look at, with my hand carefully hiding the words. But it brought back two other dates— on the torn newspaper scrap, and on the wedding invitation. All in June 1865—as if everything ran toward that certain day and month of that certain year, and then stopped; stopped forever. Silence can be eloquent, we all know, and this silence seemed to me very eloquent. Not merely of endings, but of something beyond endings; a sense of closed doors with something still behind them, something capable of being let out that shouldn't be let out. . . .

'He's asked me to marry him.'

A blankness took hold of me; when it let go I ventured, 'What did you say?'

'I told him I'd think about it.'

Another pause, while uneasy questions began collecting in me—questions I'd no right to ask. No need though, she answered without my asking.

'You're wondering whether he means it, or whether it's a . . . disarming tactic?'

'Well, something like that.'

'I don't know myself—not with a man of that type.'

There was a strange inconsistency between her cool as-
sessment of him, and her complete subjection to him.
'I'd even take him at his word and force a showdown.
Only. . . .'

'Only what?'

'—only it's driving a sharp bargain.' She grimaced.
'Who wants a shotgun wedding?'

'Christabel.' I was impatient all at once. 'For God's
sake do it or don't do it.'

'It's easy to say.'

My waspishness was all at once dissolved—rebuked—
by her look. She was staring into a void, and she was defenceless.

'He's selfish, you know, utterly selfish.'

I needn't strain myself, I answered silently, *to believe it.*

'He's used to having his own way with women, he as-
sumes he'll have it. And it's funny how he can get it just
by . . . by . . .'

She sounded just like a hurt child, bewildered at its
hurt.

'. . . by laughing at you—brushing you aside—as if
you didn't exist. He makes *you*—your feelings, your
thoughts—he makes all that a nothing.'

What does one say at these times? What's worth saying?

'I thought I'd a little strength, a few convictions. But
all that, when you're in love . . . it's not even rubbish.
You're not you any more, you're . . . you're other.'

She stared at me and didn't see me. And I, I felt an
old wound tearing open again, bleeding. But surely it
was buried by now, thickly sealed over and over with
scar-tissue? Surely I'd forgotten it by now, I didn't mind
any more . . . ?

'Just cut it off, I've told myself a thousand times over.

Just have the guts, just *stop*.' She closed her eyes. 'But when I think of never seeing him again, not ever . . .' her face was a blind mask, her voice barely a whisper, 'I think I'll die.'

Thank God for Dancey. I'd have thought him the last thing I'd ever be thanking God for, but there it was; he and his work appeared just when my sense of helplessness was crushing me toward the edge of a nervous break-down, and saved my life. My maiden commission in-volved a sumptuous brocade with exquisite linings, and if I do say it, he was in raptures. 'You're bloody marvelous, deah, I always knew it,' he twittered, and gave me a cheque then and there—a pleasant variation; plenty of well-to-do women don't scruple to keep you waiting. 'How's the old fart down below?' he carolled, departing. 'Letting off as strong as ever?'

So at least I needn't worry any more about being able to please him; nice to have a mind at rest in one direction, anyhow. And he amused me, his prancing in and out like a ballet dancer under those heavy weights of material and his vile remarks in that lisping voice; he cheered me up, I couldn't help it. So all in all my success with him, and being paid so well and so promptly, took me out of my-self a little, I mean to the point where I could sometimes shut my mind to our troubles; alone and idle, I couldn't have done it. I even found the gaps between jobs more than acceptable, the work being so extremely concen-trated. It was during these patches of uplifted spirits that I found curiosity enough—rather against expectation—to continue sampling Euphrasia's spleen; see how long I could hold out this time. But my languid curiosity must

177

have been languid indeed to dull me for so long to a word new with her, and constantly repeated. However, when I did wake up to what she called *overheard*, I could take it—without trouble—to mean continual eavesdropping.

> Something odd afoot; James and Adelaide quarrelling, in bedroom of course with door closed. Unheard of; she always the silent one yet now the louder of the two. James also loud, and *angry;* unheard of likewise, of all men he is least stirred to ill-nature.

I'm rather puzzled myself, I admit; for a wife as spiritless and obedient as Adelaide to oppose her husband persistently is an outstanding event, almost guaranteed to do what it has done—attract Euphrasia's ear to the bedroom door as often as possible. Also, the entries swell sensationally in size; by evidence of their mere length, detail and frequency she's now putting into her spying the wholehearted energy she'd put into her hate.

> I lose too many words, provoking. All the same a *dispute!* unmistakable! over the girl's *marriage-portion!* Adelaide seems to press for more?? sounds downright hysterical. James IS holding out. WHY? He can well afford to do it handsomely. Girl is his only child and he knows he must keep up his end if they wish to marry her into a rich family like the Swingles. If marriage shd not come off after all through disagreement over settlements, HOW I shd LAUGH!!

I've not the least doubt of it, dear Euphrasia. Yet she's no time to lick her chops, even over this delicious prospect;

an unforeseen threat comes forward, powerfully switching her attention from Belle to herself.

James is in MONEY DIFFICULTIES! *Must* be the reason he cannot portion the girl properly; no accounting for it otherwise. Will he try to borrow from me, next? My answer is ready; must think of myself first after all. *Shocked* at this discovery, had always taken him for very well off. Better begin looking for other lodgings quietly and at once, before he has chance to ask me for help? He with his lot of she-wastrels, fine clothes and dances etc for that girl. If reduced to poverty through waste and ostentation so be it, a salutary though severe lesson. Poor dear Adelaide, no more carriage! Has he been *speculating*?

A threat to her money, yes; how it would rouse all the vigilance of a woman like that. Moreover the dispute between husband and wife, not quite understood, spurs her unfanciful wits to unaccustomed conjecture—or even, possibly, to actual divination—?

Now I see, I understand *all*. James is bankrupt or nearly, wishes to admit it and break off match; Adelaide will not consent, insists he must stave off crash, keep up appearances till girl is safely wed, no wonder she clamours so. Pauper sister aids and abets wicked deception I doubt not. Oh those vile dishonest women, HOW I shd love to expose their scheming to bridegroom's family. Yet no *absolute* proof, am at a standstill willy-nilly. Maddening.

To find myself in agreement with the widow on any point is humiliating, but in this chief respect she's right. If Belle's father can't come up with the stipulated dowry I can well understand Adelaide's hysteria, her terror of the match falling through; Ah yes, my dear, that's how the Victorians did it. Read your Thackeray if you don't believe me, read that awful thing where he's dining with the bloated old man-about-town at his club. Oh how cruel, even at this remove of time; the hopes, the sickening suspense, the death-blow. Death quite literally for a young girl with mediocre social connections and without money; no future *is* death.

> Saw advert^mt for accommodations in Chelsea. Went over to inspect, small clean house, two good rooms. Landlady well recommended, has been housekeeper for thirty years to Lord and Lady Carwell. She takes gentlefolk only—

Ha!

> —and will study my tastes. Left deposit for rooms. Her terms rather high but money spent for comfort is well spent. Take my own bed etc, put rest in store. Have begun to sort things for packing saying no word to any. No hurry abt leaving however, am too curious to know what is in the wind. If their grand plans come to dirt, must not miss it. Wait a short while and *watch*.

Watch is one way of saying it, undoubtedly.

Nothing happens.

Dismal and all by itself, about a week later.

> No grave trouble that I can see, disappointing. The chit gay and hoity-toity as ever without a

care in the world seemingly. Yet J and A continue quarreling in secret. Still cannot make sense of it but must be *something*; cannot understand it.

A lot of vague pother it begins to sound like; pumped up into a mystery that doesn't exist, very likely, and becoming by now rather wearisome if not futile.

Hate to leave without knowing. But cannot delay indefinitely, Chelsea rooms paid for. One advantage, will avoid disgusting flummery of wedding.

Yet she's still shillying and shallying, some days after.

Delay one more week? Promise myself, this one *positively* the last. Well worth it if *any* chance of finding out—

The car door slamming brought me out of Euphrasia's contorted guess-work with a jolt. As I watched Dancey hauling long bolts of fabric out of his little van, I realized I'd forgotten he was due. Imagine it!

The bang on the hall door resounded just on one. I'd been working raptly all morning and actually was about to knock off when it came, making me—even at that distance—jump a foot. In the time it took me to rise and walk the length of the flat it'd built up to a fusillade, a furious battering. With equal fury I whipped the door open, upon the expected apparition.

'You're making too much noise with your machine,' she shot at me. 'You just stop it now, you hear?'

I gaped; not only at her manner and her strident voice but at her red congested face, her black eyes small with enmity; not so much Mrs. Rumbold as her primitive core stripped bare, if ever I saw one.

'But—' I managed, stupefied '—but it's empty underneath—'

'Tain't empty,' she bawled. 'My daughter's not so well and she's laying down, and how can she sleep with that blasted thing going overhead?'

'Well.' I'd collected myself again. 'Of course if Miss Rumbold isn't well I'll stop at once, I was just about to stop in any case.' I became haughty. 'It really wasn't necessary to hammer on the door in that manner, Mrs. Rumbold.'

'Don't you tell me what's necessary and what ain't—!'

'I *shall* tell you,' I said coldly. 'Especially since you yourself said I could use the machine as much as I liked—'

'Never mind what I said!' she shouted. 'I didn't mean you could make that bloody racket when my girl's down with headache and tryin' to get some rest!'

'I told you,' I returned glacially, 'that I would stop.'

Under her breath she muttered something uncommonly like, 'You better,' then stood there another moment, puffing and glaring. As she turned abruptly and clumped down the bare echoing staircase, she didn't look at me again.

My lunch didn't amount to much, after that; not surprising. What did surprise me, though, was the way I was taking it. Not with the loathing and contempt I'd felt when she'd been so rotten over Christabel's little housewarming, only passively, resignedly. This new demonstration of hers I linked with her blow-up over the uncarpeted stairs, just more of the same—a further outbreak of the pain and worry over her daughter that obviously gave her no rest. Her child was unhappy, mine was un-happy, and what I felt for her was a close and melancholy tie—laugh if you like—of *kinship*. I was so strangely un-resentful, so comparatively unshaken over it all, that I could actually detach my mind from the occurrence and fix it, however dispiritedly, to Euphrasia; there seemed a wry, appropriate continuity—in passing from the dead woman's harrowing unkindness to the living one's harrow-ing unkindness, and back again to the dead one's.

New idea. All by itself; now what's she up to? *Must be some way to prove; find out.*

I see; she's still on the track of some new means to prove her brother's financial embarrassments—and betray him, naturally, where it can best damage Belle's hopes. And yet I've never gathered that she had such a grudge against brother James, even; I expect it's his indulgence to Adelaide, Belle and Laurentia that's finally damned him in her eyes.

> Not easy, such matters unknown to me. Also
> grt deal of exertion, some expense certainly,
> perhaps to no avail? But think how grateful
> Swingles wld be if it were so; excellent family
> and so *rich*.

Here an interval between dates, empty even of sums; five whole blank days, like time left for something horrid to ripen.

> After enquiries, know how to go about it.
> Hackney cab to Oxford Circus 12 sh there and
> return, Atlas bus to Holborn 6d fare each way.
> Exorbitant expense, plus two short *walks* in this
> unseasonable heat. Only way however to find
> out.

Remarkable, isn't it, how ill-will can invigorate? A woman like Euphrasia—'of full-bodied habit', as they'd have described her then—I'd assume to be rather inactive. But to do her brother and his family an injury she'll walk *miles* in the sun, any day.

> Cannot make up my mind to go, grt heat continues. Plagued by thought of Chelsea rms paid for and standing empty. But plagued much worse wondering if I am right or tis only my fancy. Little time left, one way or other *must decide* QUICKLY!

Then pages and pages Oh dear, while she can't make up her mind—so boring that I gave over for the day. You see, none of all this was consecutive; I had to pick it out bit by bit from her thickets of figuring—resumed with new zeal because of her prospective removal, I imagine—plus endless mutterings about the cost of this and that. Among all that it would be easy to miss something important, if boredom and impatience tempted you to skip. But I didn't skip, not for all the world—but in this resolve there's so much . . . puzzlement, yes, *bewilderment* . . . that I've got to stop and try to reason why.

It's not on account of the woman's suffocating malevolence, nor yet of its conclusion. I know what's happened and what's going to happen, I've known all that from early on. What Euphrasia's latest ingenuity will be for revealing her brother's poverty and hurting his family through his daughter, I don't know yet and I don't much care; this detail—I feel instinctively—has nothing to do with the puzzle, it doesn't even graze its edges. The woman's been digging her own grave long since, and what finally happens is predictable—that someone's hand will push her into it. But why—

And yes! here's the answer at last, here's the core of my incomprehension—why Laurentia's hand? Insignificant creature that she is, she's long been dropped from Euphrasia's journal, forgotten and discarded for bigger and better game. How is it then that she suddenly re-appears—obscure no longer but transformed to chief character in full limelight, fatally monopolizing and dominating centre stage? I can't make it out. . . .

And shan't do either with this cotton-wool speculation, only I'm too tired to read any more. For all this isn't *consecutive*, you know; it has to be picked out bit by bit from closely-written pages and so very slowly, for fear of losing the thread. Wearisome at best, and terribly hard on the eyes after sewing.

'Lorna, now that I seem to be engaged—'

A thunderbolt; somehow I'd never really believed it would happen.

'—when can Basil take the two of us to a . . . a family dinner?'

'Oh Christabel, not yet.'

It'd got away from me, I hadn't meant to refuse like that. She didn't miss the least nuance of it either, only looked at me. And that look—its uncertain attempt to take my rejection lightly, its pretence that everything was all right, mixed with painful appeal. . . . Oh, I couldn't bear it.

'I've been a bit—' I blundered on, trying to mend matters '—a bit plowed up one way and another—'

'I know, the machine and so forth—but you're not

worrying over that any more, surely?' She looked at me, forlorn. 'So now that that's over, wouldn't you . . . ?'

A thousand awarenesses flooded through my next hesitation. She was going to marry him, apparently; I would then have to be, or seem, on easy and cordial terms with him. If I were sour and grudging and standoffish, I knew it would be a small gnawing worm in her consciousness; these knowledges are a penalty of the closeness that was between us. And I wouldn't spoil her happiness or her chance of it, I would *not*. Only . . . the man's first appearance on the scene as Miss Rumbold's lover, his casual, his *amused* acknowledgment of it—I wished I knew less about him, that's all. And again I reminded myself: *You don't count, your feelings don't count. . . .*

'What about,' I blurted, 'Thursday week?'

'Thursday week?'

'Yes. Would it be all right for hi—for Basil?'

Get it over with. My sudden right-about-face wasn't mere lack of character. *The longer I put it off the more obvious my unwillingness will be, and the more unacceptable my surrender. So, get it over with. . . .*

She heard me and understood me perfectly and submissively, and her submissiveness pierced me again. All she said though was, 'I expect it's all right for him, I'll ask him and let you know.'

'Yes, do.'

'You'll like him,' she hazarded wistfully, 'when you get to know him.'

'Of course,' I agreed too fervently. 'I know I shall.'

Later in the evening—

'Does Alec know you're engaged?' something put it into my head to ask.

'No.' She said it without looking up from her book.

Why haven't you told him? I asked silently. *Darling, why not?*

She heard me again, I'll swear to it, but she didn't answer.

I was right. I was right.

You can fairly see her drooling over the juicy morsel, whatever it is.

O that wicked woman Adelaide. O what vile deceit. Sin is a bitter husk and you have made your husband partake thereof. Yet call yourself a good wife no doubt. James equally guilty. Weakness *is* guilt. How *well* I did to suspect. Worth the cab hire, long hot bus ride among all sorts and conditions of people. Nearly a pound all told but worth every penny. O Adelaide's slyness. Not hers alone. Abomination. Well, we shall see. We shall see.

The broken sentences, breathless; so unlike her lumbering factual gait. And the nauseous excursion into evangelism isn't her style at all.

Must think what to do. Rich worthy people being cheated by outward seeming, shameful. Cannot stand by and allow it, my conscience will not suffer me. Must save these victims of falsehood, it is my duty.

You bet, Euphrasia—except that the slave to duty seems to become undecided; so much so that, fool as I am, I begin to hope. Surely, surely she'll think again? surely she can't do that cruel wicked thing to a young girl?

Cannot delay too long. Wedding-day ideal, but too late. So above all, question is—*when?* Cannot decide till I know their plans. Must bide my time. Must wait.

From here on, hot steamy puffs of two or three words.

Only wait. Guilt, yes. I know *whose.* If only they knew. If they knew.

Dark oily chucklings, like water underground.

SO. Last grand festivity for Belle in own home. Thank you for this intelligence dear Adelaide. Now I know WHEN and you yourself have told me. Yes, blind fool that you are.

I had to stop. What for I didn't realize till I straightened up; my neck and shoulder-blades were paralyzed. While taking a couple of deep breaths and letting them loosen up a bit, what I'd done—idly and unthinkingly—was to flip the page over, and get the shock of my life. The end! all unknowing I'd got to the end; overleaf was about half written on, and then no more. Had she been cut off before she could finish? in so few last lines there was surely no room for adequate revelation? A frightful blow, if true; a chill began seeping through me as I resumed, a premonitory sickness.

Have announced my departure. James silent. Adelaide all regrets and protestations, But you are leaving on very day of our last gala for Belle as an unwed girl, will you not help us receive and see all the pretty young bridesmaids etc. To her disgusting hypocrisy I reply, Very sorry but have made plans and cannot change them. She simpers, We shall miss you. I say,

Yes, Adelaide, I know how much you will miss me. Pauper leech sitting by, affects to take no notice of me. *Killing.* Laughed so hard in my room I got stomach-ache. Having to do it silently is why, not good for my health. Must contain myself. Not easy however.

A longing took me: to pull loose from her gloating, devour that last page and see whether—in fact—it ended in another of my blind alleys, another calamitous zero . . . and again I wouldn't, I wouldn't turn before it was time, I *wouldn't* cheat.

So. Two departures at one and same time almost. Mine first, then Belle's. Or remains to be seen??? One thing I am *sure* of; my last farewells at Belle's last party never forgotten easily or so I fancy. Without conceit, wonder at my own cleverness. How many women wld have got wind of this fraud, only from James holding out against settlements? Cheating tradesman that he is, no more and no less, old habits strong? Can hardly wait. What will they say, how will they look when I—

I'd whipped the page over when the noise impaled me stock still—and at the same time told me everything, the small metallic chattering and grating, the key violently thrust in the lock by a shaking hand. Even while burying the journal like a flash, even before she'd come in, I knew. I didn't need the look on her face nor the aura of calamity about her, I didn't need her failing voice to tell me, I *knew.*

'She's seen us,' she blurted. 'The . . . the daughter
. . . she saw me with Basil.'

I think I managed some sound or croak of interrogation,
or maybe not. I do remember feeling cold all at once,
deathly cold.

'He's been—driving me home rather often,' she pursued, undoing her coat in jerks. 'Never to the door of
course, just to the High Street. We—we even avoid the
bus stop, he parks well away from it before I get out.
There was—there was no reason she should be there,
where he—where he'd stopped. But she was.' She breathed
raggedly. 'There she was, all right.'

More silence from me. Say what? and what for?

'I'd just got halfway out of the car when he reached out
and took my hand and—and kissed it. And she came walking past and turned her head and looked at us. With this
absolutely blank face, no expression at all, not a flicker.
She just . . . looked.'

'She—' it came out mangled, I had to try again. 'She
didn't say *anything*?'

'I've told you, not a syllable. Didn't stop, didn't slow
down, just went on past.' She expelled another shaken
breath. 'She's told the mother by now, of course.'

Of course, I echoed—not aloud I believe, but I'm not
sure.

Meanwhile she'd walked out, carrying her coat; after a
bit I heard her putting the kettle on, and after that she
came back. I don't believe I'd moved at all; I wasn't
thinking nor feeling. Some disasters just lock you into a
vacuum, it's how this one affected me. She took a chair
in an automatic sort of way, quite recovered to all appearance, but still horribly pale. So there we both sat

with tides of cataclysm washing over our heads, till finally she said, 'She can't do anything.'

'Who can't?' I was too numbed with shock to sort out her meaning. 'The mother or the daughter?'

'Lord, who's worrying about the daughter? She's neither here nor there. It's the—the other one.'

'Yes,' I said with heart-felt conviction.

'She can't do anything,' Christabel repeated more firmly. 'So don't go worrying yourself into a flap, because she can't do a thing.'

'She can try.'

'There're ways—' she sagged with a lethal tiredness '—of taking care of that, too.'

'I hope you're right.'

'Look, darling.' She sat up straight again, reassuring and protecting me. 'Before we ever took this lease, I went to the local Rent Officer. I wanted to be clear about our situation just in case, seeing the type of person we'd have to deal with.' She produced a fair imitation of a smile. 'I've got the rights of it down pat, believe me. And the woman—she must know *something* about it, she can't try anything without getting in trouble up to the eyeballs, stupid as she is she must know that much. But if she chooses to come, let her come—I'm ready for her.'

'Oh, I realize she can't just put us on the street. But—'

'But what? Darling, I agree it's hellish luck, we've spent so much money and worked so hard, but then what? We can't afford just to get out, we've got to save again till we've enough to get out *with*. And,' she qualified, with a warlike glint in her eye, 'get out only on condition she pays us for what we've spent. You've kept the cancelled cheques, receipts—?'

'Oh yes.'

'The Tribunal can make her reimburse, you know—if we prove she's trying to drive us out.' She meant it to sound victorious, but it wasn't very successful. 'So it's we that're in a strong position, not the old harridan.'

I was silent.

'Lorna! Come on, pet, it's horrid but it can't be helped. Or—' her voice sharpened '—was there something else?'

'No,' I lied.

'There is, I can tell. Come on, tell me.'

'Nothing at all, I promise.' I managed a smile on my own account, and ghastly it must have been. 'We've enough on our plates, wouldn't you say—to be going on with?'

'Well.' She returned the smile, then was heart-broken all at once. 'I'd like to cry my heart out, that's what. Here I thought you'd a comfortable home, and even if I married—you could rent the extra room, I mean if you liked—to someone very nice—and the front garden doing so well—' her voice broke. 'I'm not crying, I'm *not*.—Oh God!' She jumped up. 'The kettle, I'd forgotten—!'

Oh those next days; like leaden weights on my shoulders. Not only weight of the situation with its loaded potential, but of the thing I'd lied about and still felt as *worst* of the situation; it hadn't yet occurred to Christabel, but it had to me. I knew that the Rumbold woman's own nature, in spite of deterrents like Rent Acts and all that, would force her to reprisals of a serious variety. I knew it in my bones, and my bones seldom deceive me. It's said that circumstance alone has power to drive you; in my experience temperament can drive you just as hard—and even more blindly—to your own disadvantage or destruction. And if you asked me if Mrs. Rumbold would cut off her nose to spite her face I'd answer you, Yes, it'd strike me as exactly the sort of thing she *would* do.

So with nerves on the stretch and ready to jump out of my skin if you looked at me, I waited. I waited for something to happen, and it didn't. Days followed, three, four, five of them, and there was nothing, absolutely nothing. And don't call it a lull either, don't think it was soothing or reassuring; beneath the unnatural quiet I could feel that ominous building-up, that muttering all but soundless, that precedes hell breaking loose. Waiting for you don't know what—it's the worst kind.

And with it other frets and rubs, like that old business of *What'll I do if we should meet?* My spying on her comings and goings had become compulsive and constant, with my own shopping timed accordingly; I began dodging in and out like a hunted rabbit. Oh yes, I'm craven, I've never denied it; in the face of trouble it's my girl that's got to stand up for both of us, especially as I've got older.

Meanwhile I did what I'd done before: flung myself on the one resource I had. I worked as if my life depended on it, I drugged myself with work till my eyes would give out and I'd hardly strength enough to rise and get away from the machine. To the question of its making noise— and this was strange—I'd stopped giving even a thought. Stranger still, I'd the firmest conviction that *she,* too, no longer bothered to notice it. For what she now wanted to avenge, she'd try to find some ground of injury far more lethal than carping about the machine. Conviction that kept raising its head higher and higher, however I'd keep shoving it to the back of my mind. . . .

Since that day of doom, Christabel and I hadn't talked about it. With the thing always in the forefront of our minds we clung tenaciously to what I can only call the

. . . the *normality* of the interior. The place was kept even more up to the mark than usual, I wouldn't let it begin looking the way we felt; with its deceptive tranquillity and comfort and brightness it made me think of a lovely ship doomed to go down . . . yet then again, believe it or not, I'd perk up. Perhaps Christabel had been right; perhaps the woman *did* know enough about rulings and regulations to realize that she couldn't attack us in force without a great deal of risk to herself.

That's how it was on this particular afternoon, at least I think that's how it must have been. It was Christabel's day off and the two of us were sitting—pleasantly, and to all appearance peacefully—over the second cup of tea.

The single knock on the door was a long way from the pounding and banging of the previous occasion, yet it was so full of determination and demand that it brought both our heads up, identically startled, at the same moment.

'I will, Christabel,' I murmured, heading her off; she'd started to rise. Not having my various experience, she couldn't know what I knew with absolute conviction: *this is it*, while I pulled the door open and said neutrally, 'Good afternoon, Mrs. Rumbold. Yes?'

'I've come to tell you we want the flat,' she threw at me. 'There's too much noise for my daughter and me, we didn't expect t'be upset like this all the time, and we want the flat.'

'Oh?' I stammered.

'Yes, *Oh*,' she mimicked. She couldn't see Christabel from where she was standing, and I wasn't asking her in, be sure of that.

'We've had a basinful and we're tired of it.' Viciously

she deployed her pretexts that did duty for real reasons. 'I warned your niece about her hippy parties, I warned you about that blasted machine of yours and what heed did you pay me, damn all. So we're willing to give you reasonable notice, but we'll thank you to get out as soon as—'

'Mrs. Rumbold,' Christabel interposed gently. She'd approached without a sound. 'I don't care for your manner, so if you could please be reasonably civilized?—Now what's this all about?'

The woman checked, visibly unprepared. This doesn't mean she failed to rally, because she did in short order—and all the more savagely for facing the culprit, the spoiler of her daughter's future.

'I'll tell you what it's all about.' She was all but grinding her teeth. 'I'll tell you, all right. We're fed up with your rumpus overhead, the both of you, and we—'

'Oh no.' Only my girl shouldn't have said it in that drawl, she shouldn't have been so openly contemptuous. 'You'll have to do much better than that.'

'And don't give me your cheek neither, I know my rights! And listenin' out of sight just now like the nasty sly piece you are—'

'Mrs. Rumbold.'

Two words not loud, not violent, but they acted like a hand clapped over the woman's mouth. In the pause following the silence, I'd glanced at the speaker and seen someone I'd never seen before; a stranger, a cold and formidable stranger.

'You don't know your rights, by the sound of you,' continued the chilling voice. 'And you don't know ours either. First of all this is an unfurnished tenancy. You can't evict us except for non-payment of rent, or using the flat for immoral purposes. If you want to try for an eviction order on one or both of those counts, go right ahead.'

'I needn't,' snarled the woman. 'I just tell the Rent Tribunal how you're always raisin' hell up here—'

'The Rent Tribunal deals with furnished premises only,' Christabel corrected mildly. 'I'm afraid the Tribunal will refer you to the Rent Officer.'

'—all right then, the Rent Officer, Miss Know-it-all—'

'—and the Rent Officer,' Christabel pursued, with the same infuriating politeness, 'will tell you that you'll have to get a court order. Then after it's served on us there's a six-month wait, that's routine. Then after that—'

'My, you have been wormin' into it, haven't you?' From ugly she'd passed to raw offensive. 'Never mind all your court order muck, I'll tell them about that God-damned machine overhead so's my sick girl can't get any peace—'

'That was only once!' I broke in hysterically. 'And I stopped working the moment you asked me! And your daughter hasn't been ill since, I've seen her going to work as usual—'

'You told my aunt,' Christabel supported my clamour, 'you told her in my presence she could use the machine as much as she liked, it couldn't disturb your daughter—'

'Shut up!' yelled Mrs. Rumbold like one demented; the reference to her daughter from Christabel's mouth was—I do believe—what sparked off the blaze beyond control. 'Never you mind about my daughter, you dirty whore, you man-grabber, it's all you are! And the little machine's what I mean she could use, the *little* one, not that bloody great thing she's got now, sneaked it in behind my back somehow—'

'It's the same machine you saw!' I outyelled her.

196

'Cow!' she topped my yell. 'Couple o' liars the both of you, it's *not* the same one I saw when I was up here that couple o' times! It's different, it's bigger—'

'It's the only machine I've ever had!' I repeated my despairing lie, at the top of my voice.

And you *see?* you see, don't you, what a fool I am, how utterly I was missing the point with my futile protests and denials? But someone else hadn't missed it, someone else had seen it in a flash and been on to it in the same flash.

'Mrs. Rumbold.' My girl's voice brushed mine aside. 'How do you know it's a bigger machine, if you've only been up here those two times?'

Silence; instant and literally deafening.

'You've been up here twice, you've just this moment finished saying it,' she pursued. 'So how can you say it's bigger than the one you saw, if you've never been up here again?'

'I—I—'

While she stammered and yawed I was waiting for her to say she knew by the sound of it, an argument not improbable. But no, she was in it up to the neck, struggling to find some way out, and her sluggish wits wouldn't oblige. No more sluggish than mine, however, missing her lethal slip that Christabel'd nailed at once.

'You must have been in our flat during our absence?' went on the inquisition, quiet and merciless. 'How else? And how often were you up here? And alone, or your daughter too?'

Cringing I waited for that incendiary *daughter* to set off another explosion, but nothing came. Demoralization isn't a pretty sight, not even the enemy's; after a moment the heavy bulk stirred, turned about and made for the stairs.

'Wait, Mrs. Rumbold,' said Christabel, not loudly. 'Wait a moment, you'd better.'

The voice always unraised but compelling, stopped the other in her tracks.

'You've been trespassing,' she pursued. 'Trespass is a legal offence. Even you know that, I expect.'

The woman was listening with her back turned square toward us; I was glad I couldn't see her face.

'Also, by what I've just been hearing, it seems you've been annoying my aunt on various pretences, just trumped-up rubbish.'

No answer.

'You'd better read up on the scale of fines they charge a landlord for harassment,' the gentle steely voice went on. 'A hundred pounds for the first offence, five hundred pounds for the second.'

No answer.

'Now the language you've been using to me I'll overlook for the present. But if ever again you dare approach my aunt with trumped-up objections and complaints, rubbish like that, I'll refer the matter both to the Rent Officer and to our solicitor, at once. You'll be the one in trouble, not we.'

In slow dragging motion the unwieldy figure began moving downstairs.

'And if you don't believe me, I advise you to see the Rent Officer yourself. Shall I—' her gentle pitiless voice followed the massive form's retreat '—shall I give you the address of our local one? I'd be glad to, if you like.'

'Fool.' Her voice rang out before the door had quite closed. 'What a fool.'

'Shhh! she'll hear—!'

'Who cares? Can you imagine anyone but an utter blunderbuss making such a slip? putting her foot in it like that?'

Her eyes were brilliant, her nostrils flaring with victory—and it all died on the instant, quenched like a candle going out. After a moment she sat down as if her legs would no longer support her.

I sat down too, and between us fell a blankness that wasn't silence.

'Thank God she still hasn't realized I'm sewing professionally,' I ventured after the long pause. 'It only needs that to light up the sky.'

'Yes,' she murmured. Her voice was both empty and remote, and with all my unhappy power of comprehension —where she's concerned—I understood. For all this wretched business with the man wasn't of her seeking nor wishing, there stood the *fact*—of injury she'd done another girl. And to have it come out nakedly as it had done: to have it flung in her face with the full vitriol of maternal rage and hatred behind it—it'd taken it out of her, and why not? As a victory it didn't make for pleasure nor rejoicing—or not so that you could notice.

I began having—shortly after this collision—the sense of being followed. Nonsense, you'll say, imaginings of near-senility, but the feeling was *there* and I couldn't shake it off; moreover it grew stronger and more persistent. I'd begun throwing hunted glances behind me, and once or twice these convulsive neck-jerkings seemed to give me a glimpse of someone dodging back hastily. I couldn't be sure, what with crowded pavements and my own slight short-sightedness, but I thought it was Mrs.

Rumbold. On Underground platforms and in bus queues I'd begin wondering if the last thing I'd ever feel, one day, would be the hard thrust at my back that would push me into the path of a train or under a thundering lorry.

I don't know, either, that you can discount *all* of it totally. My fear was rooted in my knowledge—knowledge, I repeat, not conjecture—of what the woman's state of mind must be. Her memory of the final brawl, when she'd ended ingloriously under Christabel's heel, so to speak, must be festering to the point where she was no longer responsible for her actions; where she could no more halt and weigh consequences to herself, than a mad dog. Obsession whips itself along as crazily as blindly; whether good or bad it can lash people to extremes of action uncharacteristic, unrecognizable—and unpredictable. . . . Of course I didn't just succumb to these vague terrors without a struggle, there were times when I could persuade myself it was all nonsense, overheated imagination —but also there were times when I couldn't. So what with swinging dizzily between fear and less fear and worse fear, with my dread of the forthcoming 'family dinner' filling all the cracks between—no, I can truthfully say it wasn't the happiest time in my life.

All the same, within my natural limitations, I took very special pains with my appearance for this first real meeting with Christabel's future husband. Feeling that such a man couldn't be overjoyed by his fiancée's background of elderly aunt who was a working seamstress, I'd gone all out to demonstrate to him that I wasn't *entirely* ignorant of the amenities, even of the graces. In consequence I allowed ample time to adorn myself so that I was ready rather too early, and sat at the front window, waiting. I had on my best black dinner dress, very severe and smart. I'd made it myself and I've seen no better in good shops, priced at forty pounds. On my shoulder I'd pinned a little brooch that my sister had left me, a tiny basket, real diamonds, with red and blue flowers in it; hopelessly unfashionable but I was fond of it. I had on black satin court slippers, and on a nearby chair waited my black silk coat (made it myself also) and my evening bag, black satin with cut-steel trimming. Forgive all this maundering over trifles but I *like* to remember it, especially now; I like to think of myself freshly bathed and my hair looking its nicest from my afternoon visit to the hairdresser and myself waiting in the pretty room in the precious decency— the *incredibly* precious decency—of solitude. I'd even begun feeling a slight uplift, you can't help it, you know; a nice dress and its smart little accessories and a touch of fresh fragrant scent—they do that to you, even if you aren't looking forward to the occasion. It *was* rather a bad taste in my mouth that Christabel and I had to take a taxi and meet him at the restaurant, instead of his calling for us. But the evening was so lovely, the June evening of long bright daylight and soft air, making you think of green country, wide and quiet and green. . . .

Was it that peaceful moment, do you suppose, that helped me to see—*see* irrevocably—what I hadn't seen before? That this marriage, however it appeared to me, was Christabel's single hold on life at this present time, and that losing a love that's wrong or destroying can cripple you as fatally as losing a love that's right and life-giving. So right or wrong her only present salvation was in marrying this Manderton, unless I wanted to see some part of her dying, or at best going warped. And that I couldn't endure, not the one any more than the other, I didn't want to live with anything like that before my eyes. So suddenly—seeing it in that lightning-stroke of clarity—I was as much *for* the marriage as I'd been against it; I was fierce all at once, defensive, full of ready-made hatred and incipient violence against anyone or anything that might impede it. And if it turned out badly, at least she'd have had a brief radiance from it, and if deceptive radiance, what of it? Some happiness that you see later as a mistake—later also it turns out to be the only happiness you've ever had, perhaps, the only moments when you've lived; so in spite of everything you know you were right to seize them.

So for her sake the marriage had to go on, *it had to be.* If a mistake, at least it'd be *her* mistake, and that's a major point too. Misfortune through your own fault you can bear, but misfortune through other people's interfering and meddling, however well-intentioned—yes, *that's* what you can't ever accept, that's what never stops rowelling you with unforgiveness and gnawing, unabating resentment. . . .

My eye fell on my watch; I came out of my revolvings with an immediate shock. On the heels of shock, came the first qualm of fear. I never worried when she was reasonably late, she was delayed sometimes, but she wouldn't let it happen with this date; she'd planned to be home by six at the worst, and it was now seven-thirty. So what could . . . what could . . . panic began gibbering in me, cold dizzy sickness shaped all at once to new horror—of *belated* understanding. Not I but Christabel pushed beneath the lorry; not I but Christabel broken, mutilated under a bus or Underground train. . . .

Just as my head was getting tight enough to snap a taxi dashed up, Christabel tumbled out, thrust money at the driver and pelted up the walk. I had the door open and she came tearing through with a gasp of 'Sorry, sorry—!' She was wrenching off her coat and talking breathlessly. 'A mass of old silver just got dumped on us out of the bank vaults—I had to get it to the Goldsmiths and Silversmiths, we couldn't risk having it in the shop overnight, and Alec'd had to go early. And then I couldn't get on a bus, all packed out—and no taxi for ages, not for love or money, and the traffic *fiendish*—!' She snatched up her coat. 'I've rung Basil, he's put our booking forward. Only now—' she gulped for breath, and she needed to '—now he's going to pick us up around the corner. Taxis are hopeless at this time of evening, I didn't want us to be another hour late. Sorry I've hung you up all this time—you do look nice, darling!' She vanished at a run.

Aaah! that was a giant sigh of relief. Then on cotton legs I tottered to my chair and fell into it. These false alarms that leave you a rag; worse, that indicate by their destructiveness how a real calamity would destroy you . . . Oh dear Oh dear. I just sat for a while, limply. And when I'd recovered somewhat—will you believe it—I was *angry*; angry with Christabel for giving me such a scare, angry that she'd dragged me into this engagement. My small mood of festivity was completely spoiled, my desire of co-operation scattered to the winds, I felt prickly and quarrelsome. A good thing I'd time to compose myself while she dressed; it would take her half an hour at least. But that long? eternity or good as, a torment of fidgets after my torment of waiting . . . I couldn't just sit, I had to do *something*, any distracting snatch to tide me over.

How I *wished* now I hadn't finished Mrs. Hepplewhite's journal. Or—

—or, actually, had I? For if you'll believe me, I couldn't remember. The cruel shock that had intervened, the mountainload of impending trouble, had knocked album, letters and journal as completely as if they'd never existed; when I thought how all that nonsense had been my one object in life, not long ago either, I couldn't credit it. Still, now that I came to think, I'd a slightly different impression: that I'd got so nearly to the end of Euphrasia's burblings that there was nothing more to learn, the few words left couldn't signify. She was clearing out bag and baggage, was my hazy recollection? while planning some furtive way of betraying her brother's poverty to the parents of Belle's intended. And come to think, where *was* the poisonous little tome? it seemed ages ago since I'd seen it. . . .

Groping in my workbasket, I found it where it'd always been buried. The mere presence of its shredded binding and mouldy smell brought back, like a blow, the key stammering in the lock, Christabel coming in to say the Rumbold girl'd seen her; Christabel pale as ashes and hardly able to get the words out. No wonder I'd blanked out, there'd been sufficient reason. Where, actually, had I broken off reading? I'd have to go back and pick up the thread. . . .

> . . . One thing I am *sure* of; my last farewells
> at Belle's last party never forgotten easily or so I
> fancy. Without conceit, wonder at my own
> cleverness. How many women wld have got
> wind of this fraud, only from James holding
> out against settlements? Cheating tradesman
> that he is, no more and no less, old habits

strong? Can hardly wait. What will they say, how will they look, when I—

Yes, it was there that I'd stopped, just in the act of turning the page.

> —when I walk in, my bonnet and shawl proclaiming that I am shaking the dust of this house off my feet forever, and say in ringing tones, "Ladies and gentlemen, I must bid you farewell. I cannot remain here to countenance, by my presence, the scandalous cheat that is being practised on an upright and unsuspecting family— the palming off, as Miss Burridge, of the nameless bastard (point at Belle) of an unmarried woman (point at old maid). Let anyone read in Somerset House that Mr. and Mrs. James Burridge have never had a child, and that *Miss* Laurentia Tisdall has indeed had one."
>
> NB. Have pondered long over these words. Without conceit find that they say all and are judiciously and well expressed.

Silence. Measureless, endless silence of being locked, immured, in realization. *Laurentia*, came soundlessly from far off. *All the time it was Laurentia, only Laurentia.* Forgotten, I'd thought? dropped by Euphrasia for more important targets? There'd been no other target from first to last; never had Euphrasia's eye left her only and single objective. In everything she'd done—how clear it all was in retrospect, how cruelly clear—she'd been worming toward her goal; every set-to over Belle, climaxed by the slapping incident, had all had the one purpose—to promote conflict with Laurentia, to pile up aggravation till her situation was intolerable and she was driven from the house. That, only that, had been the aim all along. And why? why this rooted hatred of the rich and secure woman for the one who had nothing? Instinctive knowledge of inferiority is all I can guess—the widow's perception of her own mean soul in the presence of Laurentia's fine one—of all grudges the most blindly destructive, unforgiving and malignant. Euphrasia's indirectness of manoeuvre had misled me, that was all; her deviousness that I couldn't see when it was under my nose. . . .

And the old lady, the recluse dying alone in the decaying and neglected house—the old lady was Belle, pretty Belle. Shamed, branded and humiliated before her circle, you might say her whole social world; the match broken off, whether by her intended husband's initiative or his family's compulsion; shrinking into concealment, withering among ponderous Victorian drapes and furniture gradually smothered and eaten by dust; living on cruelly till 1930 and dying in squalor; that had been the end of Belle so young and pretty in her latest dashing finery. And—by the flaring bad-smelling gaslight that illumined those decades—you'll see that her story couldn't have ended otherwise. Remember the morality of the day, as rigid as hypocritical, and never more so than among the lower middle classes. Remember the pitiless exclusions, the former friends cutting her dead after her public branding as a bastard, followed by the worse scandal of murder and suicide; the party breaking up in horror and chaos, and James Burridge lying his valiant best in the coroner's court to hush it up. But who in all Clapham wasn't chewing it over joyfully, twenty-four hours later?

I don't know, either, what Belle could have done but hide. A girl of social position in what they called the

Upper Ten, above all an heiress, could have disappeared on the Continent and married well enough there; or even a girl of Belle's own class, tougher and more brazen, could have fought her way through it somehow. But this girl, inheriting from her mother a fatal sensitivity—a disabling fineness and gentleness of fibre—went down under it. And long after, with Clapham changing from a village to a suburb and then to mere packed-out London, and the story long forgotten—by then she was old, warped and deformed with hiding; out of touch and wanting to burrow always deeper and deeper, away from faces and voices and away from the light. . . .

An odd question touched me from some remoteness. Where in the house had it happened, exactly? Just where had the two women faced each other for the last time? In the room where they were dancing? In the dining-room with its heaped buffet and special-occasion champagne? At precisely which spot put X, to show where the widow confronted the spinster and saw all at once what was in the spinster's hand? It'd happened in the house, I could almost swear; Laurentia pursuing the fat woman into the garden was something they couldn't have concealed. *In* the house had been flung, across pre-bridal festivity, the dark spatter of blood, the dark after-taint and smell of drifting smoke. All on the warm evening, the sweet June evening of a century ago. . . .

'He had a pair of them,' said a harsh voice; I'd jumped, actually jumped, at the sound. The words came from me but not from my intention, not from my knowledge, not even from any thought of the sleeper under the leaves in the attic. No murder weapon, which I'd somehow always known; only the murder weapon's twin, which I hadn't ever known. But I knew it now because it told me so, the thing that . . . Oh God . . . was sweeping down on me like a wall of water, spinning me down and under and away, away . . . it was the scare over Christabel's lateness that had done it; left me empty and limp and without power to resist. At least, thinking of it later, that's how it seemed to me.

Christabel'd returned. She must have bathed and dressed in record time, but to save my life I couldn't tell you how she looked or what she had on. I suppose she helped me into my coat, and after that we were in the street, walking; I've literally no memory of going downstairs or leaving the house. Some vague curious things though I do remember, such as my sense that she was hustling me along and my faint sleep-walking irritation at it, and I remember the words that came nearly as far as my lips: *Belle, my love, pray not so fast!* only I didn't say them. Long afterward I asked her if she'd noticed anything strange or different about me, but wasn't surprised when she said no—seeing the poor lamb must have been under too considerable strain herself to notice much, more worried and nervous than she'd admit over the forthcoming 'family' occasion.

I can't describe my state either, even to myself; I've tried and tried. First I thought of it as a falling, an endless falling into endless dark, only it's not that at all. Nor is it like going under anaesthetic, that swimming and lifting away from yourself; I fancy it's more like those frightful brain operations where you've got to remain conscious in order to guide the surgeons, and they touch one and another part of the brain and your arms and legs move, it's not you that's moving them yet it *is* you, it's a force inside you and yet outside. It's not hypnosis or anything to do with it either, I'd swear, though hypnosis may be an outermost threshold of what I'm trying to define. Only with it I imagine there'd be no terror, no sense of this . . . this *Other* . . . that dislodges you and takes over your shell for its own uses, against all your volition. . . . Oh dear I can't, it takes powers beyond mine to describe it. Or—is it an intimation of the end, a hint of what it will be—the final obliteration of *you?*

Duke! Duke! death is terrible, death is very terrible!

You remember it, Ann Hyde's awful cry in her last moment? She knew, then; *she possessed the knowledge of the last,* only she couldn't communicate her knowledge. No more can I communicate the knowledge of my lesser extinguishment—by what had been trying to fasten on me from the moment Mrs. Rumbold opened her street door to us, that'd been groping about me ever since, trying to get hold, till little by little it'd dug in, established its grip, its . . . yes . . . *possession.* . . .

Meanwhile we'd almost got to the High Street with its heavy traffic, swollen now with the evening rush toward amusement; it reached me from eternities away but it did reach me, for drowning in that Other survive tiny awarenesses of your own, of *you,* and somehow this heightens your dizzy plunge down the sheer of otherness and makes it still more cataclysmic; I don't know why, but at least with me it's so. Well, as I say, we'd got to the High Street and turned the corner. He was parked a good cautious distance up the road and didn't see us at once. But I could see him, the sleek handsome man beside the sleek handsome car, both remote as through a telescope's wrong end but preternaturally distinct. . . .

At sight of him, I *knew*. With old chilling knowledge I knew what waited, I'd met it before and with frenzied panic wanted not to meet it again. *Oh no,* I was moaning and panting voicelessly, *Oh no, Oh please God no.* . . .

He'd seen us; he started advancing with his hand out and a smile of dutiful pleasure on his face. Again I could see, peering through some pinpoint rift in my terror, that he'd little difficulty in suppressing any excess of rapture. We were within a pace of him now, my lips spreading stiffly in a smile, my hand extended and all but touching his. . . .

A shriek exploded behind me. Or if not a shriek, I don't know what; a yell of hate and vindictive laughter combined, a deep-lunged, ugly malignity. The three of us, our attention naturally wrenched towards the sound, were staring at its source. With shock and amazement on Christabel's part and on his, yes, but not on mine. *It's come* was all I thought, with endless acceptance but even more endless recognition. *It's come.* She was standing a few feet behind us, her naturally red face livid, her arms flailing in manic gesticulation as flying words and flying saliva spit from her distorted mouth.

'All right!' she screeched. 'All right, *Mister* Manderton, my girl wasn't good enough for you, ha? Not good enough, why, you're not fit to tie her shoes, you dirty little sod. So you wanted better, ha? Like her, ha?' She pointed. 'Her? *her?* don't make me laugh.' A snarling laugh burst out of her, a spluttering triumph. 'All right, ask her who she is! Go on, whyn't you ask her, your Miss *Better?* Calling herself that old cow's niece—' her finger stabbed at me '—her bastard, that's more like it, that old bag's bastard kid. Go and look it up same's I did if you don't believe me, see if Mister 'n' Missis Mortimer-Warne had any kids ever! Go and see, I dare you! Them two bitches planning it all cozy, puttin' it over—on who, ha? makin' the mug of who? The mug, the mug, the mug—!'

On a final shriek she broke off, wheeled, and started to run heavily.

From now on, if it's all in splinters and jags like broken glass, you must forgive me. I know the woman disappeared, and I know the Other—in my body—set off in silent hungry pursuit, like an animal after prey. I remember my dull surprise—*mine*, not the Other's—that a woman so big and heavy could move so fast. I know too that, while my eyes never left her, I'd no sense that she moved, only that she dwindled; my eyes nailed her as she scrambled unwieldily up the steps and disappeared into the house. . . .

That much, I can tell you. What I can't tell you is whether Christabel ever had me in sight during that nightmare wafting, but it must be that I'd got into the house before she could see me. Whatever delayed her had given me the one single thing I needed—a good start of her. Whether mere shock had disabled her from following me at once, or whether she paused to make some incoherent excuse, poor lamb, I don't know at all. No, she couldn't have seen me, for then she'd have called after me; the sound of her voice might—even then—have broken through and freed me from that Other.

So then, I was in the house. Steps went up and up before me, steps without end, and up them I went with a body weightless as air. A new voice inside me was saying all at once, *Yes, Euphrasia, yes. Now, now, now,* a small voice, ladylike, and so gentle it turned me cold. *Now,* it never stopped saying, *now, now,* as I reached what hid the sleeping Babe in the Wood and began clawing and digging down toward it. Ruthlessly I woke it from its sleep under the dry rustling leaves, the Babe cold and clammy and startlingly heavy in the hand, and carried it down the attic stairs almost to the foot. Just within its door I paused, knowing I must be careful now; careful and clever and very, very sly. Christabel was home; faintly I could hear her, *Lorna! Lorna!* the sound fading and coming back again as she ran from room to room. After a few moments *Lorna!* came from the outside hall in the failing voice that was half sob, half shout. Then she'd clattered down the noisy bare steps and the street door slammed violently; she'd run outdoors to look for me, poor child.

Yet I'd no thought even for her. I wanted her away, I willed her to go. The house just to myself and to that other one, it's all I wanted. On the slamming of the door I was down the next flight, swift, quiet, down and down and down, and in the ground floor hall I began shouting, 'Euphrasia! Euphrasia!' The shouting voice that also wasn't mine seemed alien, yet infinitely familiar. And all the time she kept calling, the woman dead for a hundred years calling another woman dead for a hundred years, and naturally Mrs. Rumbold came charging up from the basement to investigate the stranger's voice shouting for a stranger. The one glaring look and furious '*Well!*' that burst from her were all she'd time for, till she saw what was in my hand. A scream tore from her then, hideous, then came a roar that wiped out the scream. But like the eye of the tempest holding unbroken quiet, the deafening roar held at its heart a deafening stillness, and again within this stillness a dying fall of *Here, it happened. It happened here, here.*

Well, that's that. What followed is still confused in my

mind, any sorting out I do is haphazard. The old revolver was picked up off the floor, flung there by what's playfully known as the 'kick'. I'd felt that kick all the way to my shoulder and it tore—literally tore—the Babe from my hand; my palm and wrist were one painful bruise for days after. Still, they tell me I was lucky that an old unused weapon like that hadn't exploded and taken off half my lower arm. And I *was* lucky, and I'm grateful; maimed or one-handed I'd have been a burden on Christabel forever. Also I was lucky that my one bit of perjury during the trial—that I'd found the gun among the effects of my late brother-in-law, Christabel's so-called father—held up perfectly well, and even luckier that I wasn't being tried for murder. For my victim hadn't died, Oh no, not she; it's only the badly needed ones, the good and the kind and the intelligent, who die. What with my maiden effort of marksmanship and the weight of the Babe and the upward wrench of the kick, the shot had gone high and only grazed her shoulder. So now she's good as new or better than new, if that's any recommendation.

But the kindness that's been shown to me here, the *kindness!* Six months I consider a light sentence for the crime I'd committed. I'm allowed to have writing materials and I'm librarian of the prison library, also forewoman in the sewing room. I get on perfectly well with my girls there, and if I find some of them frightening, well, their faces are the reflection of the lives they've had. I've even got a cell to myself, and I know they're pressed for room. Our Governor is a dedicated woman, and I'm dedicated to repaying the confidence she's shown in me from the first.

Other moments from the nightmare keep returning to me in zigzags of dark and light and out of sequence. The strange moment in court, for example, when it came out that Mrs. Rumbold hadn't bought the house, as she'd told me; she'd got it by inheritance. Exactly why she lied can't be known, but I could hazard a guess. Because she'd heard some garbled family account of tragic doings in the house, her muddy wits would see it as a threat to renting. So apparently she'd decided to conceal it from possible tenants, as in fact she'd done with us—till that moment when spite got the upper hand of her and she let it slip out. *But*: since she'd inherited, it follows she was somewhere in line of descent from the original family, the Burridge side judging by her resemblance to Euphrasia; she could have been grand-daughter or great-grand-daughter to one of Euphrasia's children. Two or three generations, you know, can easily span a century.

Then there were the moments when Alec Sterrett came to the rescue, a tower of strength before, during and after the trial; making all arrangements, providing courage where there was no courage. I was apathetic but Christabel was utterly devastated, not only with shock but bewilderment; utterly unprepared for cataclysm, since she'd no idea —then or since—of what was building up to it underground. What would we have done without his warmth and steadiness, that warmth of having a friend who was *there*, dear dear Alec.

And then, and then: the moment when Christabel flung her arms about me and said, 'Mummy, mummy.' Her whisper was strained and harsh, her whole body trembling. 'Why didn't you tell me, you fool, why didn't you tell me?'

'I didn't want—I didn't want—'

'—to spoil my chances? Oh my dear idiot, I'll spoil my own chances thank you, I don't need help. But never mind, never mind.' She hugged me more painfully. 'Everything'll be out of that bloody house and into store in two twos, and when—by the time—I mean, when—'

The tactful phrase evaded her and she gave up hunting it.

'It'll be all right, you'll see, darling, it'll be all, all right—' her incoherent murmuring broke off suddenly. 'Were you worrying about the great Basil affair?' She laughed. 'He couldn't wait to disappear—I needed that kick in the teeth to wake me up. So everything's fine, darling, couldn't be better.'

She was gay over it, excessively so. But what can you do in a case like that but hold your tongue, just be *quiet?*

When she comes to see me on visiting days, they don't throw us into the regular room, which I understand is a pandemonium horror beyond belief—crowds of people screaming and mouthing at each other through two barriers of steel mesh some feet apart, with warders pacing up and down between. No, they give us an interviewing cubicle to ourselves, and Christabel sits on one side of a broad heavy table and I on the other. The attendant wardress is practically on top of us, the place being so small, but she's quite welcome to hear anything we say; the comparative privacy is a marvelous favour, and I'm only too grateful.

Well, on one such day, suddenly Christabel said, 'Oh by the way, when I was packing I found that sweet old album you had in your wardrobe, wrapped up like a dark secret.'

'It was filthy,' I said indifferently, paralyzed that I'd say too little or too much.

'Oh no, it was clean enough.'

'Well naturally, I'd brush it up a *little* before putting it in my wardrobe, wouldn't I?' I returned mildly. 'I only meant, where it came from was filthy.'

'A junk shop?'

'More or less.'

'It's a very nice example though, in good condition—I've been looking through it. There's a family group so stuffy and Victorian it isn't true, and they're sitting in front of one of those typical period houses, sort of like the Rumbold castle. Did you notice it?'

'Too much began happening just then,' I shrugged. 'Too many things on my mind, if you know what I mean.'

'I can't imagine,' she smiled grimly. 'But in these pictures, three or four of them actually, there's a party with a big bust and a mean jaw, sort of a Rumbold type, then there's a poor puffy thing always hanging on to a thin one, and this thin old girl has the sweetest intelligent face—appealing. And whom do you think she reminds me of?'

'I can't imagine,' I said with perfect honesty.

'Of you. Especially when you're wearing certain expressions—she's the image of you, practically. I've packed the album very carefully, I wonder if you'll agree when I show you—about the resemblance.'

Don't pack it away, I screamed inwardly. *Get rid of it for God's sake, before they all get out again!* But not being able to say it, I knew that its destruction must wait on the day of my freedom. Not all that far off, but too far.

And well, well; they do say that people don't know how their own voices sound, so it may be that they don't know how they really look. Women at least, in my experience, tend to think either too well or too badly of their appearance. But I only settled to thinking of that after she'd said goodbye to me till next time, my daughter—

Heavens: I'd got so used to calling her my niece, I'd

taken such desperate care to *think* of her as my niece for
fear of some slip, that I couldn't have realized the power
of those other two words—how eloquent they are, how
marvelously beautiful, especially when you see them written.

I'll write them again.

My daughter.

I've a good bit of time to myself, what with our very
early lights-out, and all day I look forward to that exquisite
luxury of being *alone*. Not that I'm anxious to sleep after
I've got to bed, I can't spare the time for sleep; I lie there
awake in every fibre, trying to understand *what happened*.

Because—forgive me for reminding you again—no one,
no one but myself knows about the things I dug up out of
the attic and what I dug up out of them; no one knows of
what I called into being, step by step, like an evil spell
conjured up and having—once begun—to work itself out
to the end. My trial was held in a minor court with no
jury because I pleaded guilty; my solicitor described my
offence as arising from long harassment and provocation.
You could see how dull and distasteful the magistrate
found it, a stupid tenant-wrangle with a more disorderly
termination than usual.

Even Christabel hasn't an inkling of the truth. How
could she, utterly unaware as she was of my sneaking and
ferreting? She accepts my solicitor's rational and sym-
pathetic excuse for the outrage I committed, and yet—and
yet—I can see there're gaps in the story that she can't make
out, she can't understand my deed in relation to her
knowledge of my nature. And no wonder; I can't understand it myself. I shall though; I'm *determined* to understand it.

For this is the task I've set myself in my sleepless hours: to puzzle it out, to force some sort of logic—some form or design—on what came to life out of old dead dust and reached into the lives of the living. *Are you asleep, Count Magnus? Are you awake, Count Magnus?* Yes, in my indecent curiosity I disturbed something that was better left undisturbed, I opened that album and invited five dead people out of it, letting them become more and more real till they, not I, were dominating and shaping events. One can't think back in *exact* sequence all these months later, but tell me: is it just my fancy that whenever I'd read of something happening in the letters or the journal, almost the same thing happened to Christabel and me? An implacable sequence, or no, not that exactly, I don't know what to call it—

Or yes! yes, I do know: we were the *echo*. We echoed the journal exactly but more and more faintly, a fading repetition as it were, less cruel and less lethal. For example, where Laurentia killed her tormentor, I hurt ours only slightly; where Euphrasia's disclosure destroyed Belle, Mrs. Rumbold's was far from destroying Christabel. And where Laurentia killed herself, did I also intend . . . ? And the answer is yes, I did intend; I was hungry for the woman's obliteration and hungrier for my own, I was avid for healing oblivion and peace. I'd have done it too, carried the pattern out faithfully, if the gun hadn't wrenched itself from my hand and left my arm paralyzed with pain to the shoulder. So isn't it as though the evil that impelled the earlier calamity—the evil demonstrably willing to be woken—had lost its force over the years, gone weaker and weaker?

And come to think: don't our very names, even, slightly echo the journal's names? Clare Annabel has an off-key chime of Christabel, Mrs. Rumbold's maiden name—will you believe it—proved to be Burridge, and surely Laurentia Tisdall is near enough to Lorna Teasdale? And something else I'd forgotten till now: my grandmother, who was born in 1830 and lived to be over ninety, and who took a great interest in 'family' as people of that day did, once told me we'd cousins in Norfolk who spelled their name Tisdall. So the intense interest I took in Laurie, the intimate and affectionate concern I felt for her—did part of it in fact come from what I couldn't suspect, the tie of blood? Strange if true, though by no means the strangest of all the strange business.

For all this, again, isn't nearly the end of it. Like that single moment years ago when I could look at an ordinary house with utter unrecognition, I've become stripped of recognition in myself, stripped of the everyday trust in appearances that every person must have, if he wants to feel ground under his feet. Myself though, I've no trust any more; I'm certain of nothing, not now. For tell me: what power was at large in that house, that it could mutilate three people's lives according to a pattern over a century old, a pattern long vanished and forgotten? And did this pattern originate with Euphrasia, or was she too merely repeating an older one, and handing it down to us in turn?

Does anything that begins, really ever end?

Nor can I talk to the person I'd confide in naturally, without exposing my systematic grave-robbery—for that's what it was, and I'm now paying the penalty, and serve me right. I'm uprooted, alone in my eviction. Who was it that said we were so eternally deceived by *a thin veil of matter* that we never really know what—or whom—we were looking at? And I tell you it's frightening, it's terrifying, to be torn loose from every certainty you've taken for granted since birth and left groping in a waste where you're certain of nothing at all, and least of all certain of. . . .

Which brings me to the worst, the very worst. I mean, since our actions proved to be shadows of actions that had gone before; since our very names were shadows of names forgotten a hundred years and over; isn't it as though those vanished beings—call them souls, spirits or what you like —could project themselves so as to compel living flesh and blood to walk, with uncanny similarity, in their vanished footprints? And if so, mightn't it follow logically that our landlady was Euphrasia Burridge Hepplewhite, born over again? that Christabel was Belle? that I myself was Laurentia Tisdall? In this subtle blending where one loses sight of identity, tell me, who were the shadows? They, the apparently dead? or we, the apparently living?

Because there are *evidences*, you know, of these mysterious powers. Who is there in the world that hasn't been touched, however indirectly, by premonition, precognition, *déjà vu*, those million impalpable filaments from another world, invisibly all about us? What of involvements still stronger, perhaps never told—till too late? For it's well known that such experiences unfortunately impose a *silence* on those who have had them, an unwillingness to speak of them, or at least I've always heard that this is a common characteristic. My own minor but actual contacts with that other world bear this out (one involving a medium and two a pet dog, the same dog) but like most people I've never spoken of them; I didn't because I couldn't. And this reticence plus the lapse of time between the occurrence and its narration is dangerous if not fatal to *truth;* for it encourages one to believe it never happened, it makes you put it all down to imagination—whereas it wasn't imagination at all.

And just to prove to you how many, many people are still so enmeshed in this invisible web that they're driven to seek protection from it: the Church itself contemplates a . . . crash course, if you must be jocular . . . in exorcism, almost entirely disused for years and regarded by most as a colourful strand of medieval Catholicism. Yes, in this very April of this seventh decade of the twentieth century, such a contemplated step has been published in the gravest pundit among newspapers. And the initiative hasn't come from the Church; it's been driven, literally forced to do this by 'the disturbing number of requests for help' from people caught up, with bewilderment or fear, in something they don't understand. Are *all* those people ignorant, credulous or hallucinated? are they *all* liars, every one of them? Well, there's no answer but individual opinion—and a broken reed that is, as we know or should know.

Still, despite all this if you like, brush it aside; it's been so corrupted and discredited by fakery that I can't blame you. Call this world real if you like, call our bodies real, I've no quarrel with that either. We need lies for our support, we bitterly need them, and if you're able to see the lie as reality—more power to you then, and I envy you; it's after all a question of doing the best you can for yourself, isn't it.

So here I am, on a knife-edge of something worse than dislodgment: of *imminence*. I feel as though I were on some sort of threshold that I'm . . . that I'm just about . . . to step over. And Oh God I don't want to step over, I'm afraid. *Many other things I could tell unto you, but ye cannot bear them.* And yes, like the lowest one of those tired hungry mobs that trailed after Him, my ignorant self longs to remain ignorant.

But say I've settled down in my warm cozy mud, with eyes and ears and mind plastered shut against knowing; it's still not enough for day to day existence in this world. The experience in that house—James Burridge's or Mrs. Rumbold's, it's all the same only strung a little apart on the thread of time—that experience has *dispossessed* me, body and soul, and let the final banishment overtake me. I'm not *of* this world any more, but no more am I of that other one we don't know; only hung between them in space, a whistling coldness and homelessness beyond belief. Once I was comfortable company for myself, but no more. How can you sit in comfort with an identity you're not sure of? And if not sure of your own, how much more unsure of other people's? Even with those I know well; even with that single solitary being that I love; I keep thinking, *You look like someone I know, but who are you actually?*

For it would help me, it would help me so immeasurably if only I could outrun the immeasurable alienation, escape the chasm yawning with a darkness as ageless and remote as the first man, the lonely pitiless enigma: What are we? and why? and who?

Who are we?